Should

Sean Boling

Published by Sean Boling, 2019.

SHOULD

First edition. January 4, 2019.

Copyright © 2019 Sean Boling.

ISBN: 979-8224513246

Written by Sean Boling.

•••

Then I tried on a conquistador helmet.

Old Libby had a garage full of costumes from her days on the board of directors of the local community theatre. Some were from shows they had put on, others from cast parties.

"Man of La Mancha?" I asked.

"Probably," she said, bracing herself in the doorway that led to her kitchen.

"You don't remember?"

"We didn't do it," she cleared her throat, as she did every several words. "But it was in the shop, so somebody must have. Before my time."

"There's no such thing as before your time."

She flipped me a very shaky middle finger.

"No collection is complete without a conquistador helmet," she mused in a bottomless rasp that made her words sound eternal.

When she cleared her throat I told her maybe she shouldn't anymore.

"You sound so deep when you keep it raspy."

"Deep alright," she cracked. "Like I'm drowning. In my own saliva."

"One sentence too many, Libby."

I centered my head in the screen of my camera that perched on a pile of boxes aptly labeled "old photos" in Libby's handwriting, which faced the makeshift photography studio I had assembled from a clothesline and wallpaper swatches. The current sample that hung from the line was a jungle pattern. I lowered my chin and tried to rehash the same weary stare I had adopted for all the previous shots and pressed the remote in my hand. The flash kicked in.

"Dammit," I blinked away the spots that the light left behind. "Getting too dark in here. I guess it's time to call it a day."

"Does the picture look okay?"

"Way too bright," I could tell before I even held it in my hand. "He's supposed to be trudging through the jungles of South America, under a canopy of trees blocking the sun. In fact, I should spray some water on myself before I take it tomorrow. I imagine those guys were wet pretty much the whole time."

"You look miserable enough," Libby remarked as I showed her the product.

"I'm going for apathy," I reminded her. "I guess I need to lighten it up. My expression, that is."

"Everyone always makes a funny face when they try these things on."

"This is funny."

"It is?"

"I know it's almost dinner time, Libby, and you're hungry, but I told you. It's for my book that nobody's downloading."

"The one about the guy who lives forever."

"And he doesn't like immortality very much."

I removed the helmet and put it on the washing machine next to the doorway where Libby hunched.

"I would think he'd be happy."

"He has his reasons," I gave her a variation on the doleful look my character wore in the photo series. "You haven't read it, either, have you?"

"I can't read things on a screen. If it was a real book..."

"It's free, Libby. You couldn't even download it to give my numbers a bump?"

"Free?" her voice raised above a rasp.

"Every artist you ever worked with never made a dime."

"The director and choreographer got a stipend."

"Probably about as much as you pay me."

"You don't even cook," she waved me off as she turned around and shuffled to the kitchen.

"You won't let me."

I kept an eye on her while she cooked one of her five signature dishes to make sure she didn't cause a fire. I didn't even have to see or smell it to know it was three-bean casserole, since that day was always in between French bread pizza day and mushroom quesadilla day.

As she stirred a pot full of baked, kidney, and garbanzo beans, I thought about her contention that immortality should breed happiness.

"Would you want to live forever?" I asked.

"Sure."

"Really? I mean, look at you."

She chuckled, like I knew she would. She was by far the most affable of the elderly I had worked for. Many of them were just as sharp mentally, but being the least physically infirm gave her a distinct advantage in my rankings. She wasn't as embarrassed or frustrated by her condition as the others, and forced to bark out orders on how to keep her comfortable. She still had the aches and pains that come with an older body, but brokered a kind of peace between herself and her decreasing cells. I sometimes wondered aloud why she even hired me, and her answer was always the same. She wanted someone around in case of emergency, and preferred human companionship to a bracelet with a button on it.

"I would be in my forties," she said. "That was my sweet spot."

"That's about the age of my character."

"It's a good age. Right in the middle."

"Nobody else you knew in your forties would be immortal. They'd grow old and leave you behind."

"That's their problem."

I waited to see if she would reconsider, now that she was thinking about it.

If she was thinking about it.

"Kids are more into it than adults," I prodded.

"Is it a children's book?"

"No. They're more into living forever. Nobody is into my book. Ask a kid if they want everlasting life, they say yes without hesitation. Ask an adult, they recoil and say no, usually 'God no.'"

"How many people have you asked?"

"It's a small sample size," I admitted. "Maybe a dozen adults, a half-dozen kids, grandkids of people I work for mostly. But everyone's responses are remarkably uniform. Except yours."

"It's the kid in me."

She lowered the heat under the pot to a simmer and smiled.

The immortal can't remember being a child. He's been an adult for hundreds of lifetimes and thousands of years. He doesn't know how old he is, neither the age he is perpetually living nor how many years he has been on Earth. He thinks of himself as middle-aged. He thinks of his life in sections, rather than an endless line, which doesn't make the sections any more memorable. People can't recall being a baby within their own lifetime. The immortal is no different, and his lifetime spans human history. The brain fills up and clears space for new information. Memories without any significance are the first to go. Which makes him wonder about the lives he's lead. He wonders if his memories have been absorbed into lessons and skills, or if they were simply not worth saving. He is very handy. He knows he has helped build enough structures and plant enough gardens to fill a large city and its suburbs because his occupational instincts are so evolved. He barely needs to use levels, squares, protractors, and tape measures. He has journal entries that stretch back a few hundred years. When he reads them he feels as though he's reading something written by someone else. They are in a composition book that he bought in 1912. The first line reads, "Entries I can remember from the pages lost in the fire." But he doesn't expand on "the fire", where it happened, or how. He must have assumed when he wrote it that he would always remember what it meant. He should have known better by then, having lost so many memories. It probably has something to do with a vision he still has of a building he watched burn. It was over a hundred years ago, so the memory only flickers for a second. It may have been two hundred years ago. Maybe the entry is a metaphor, and there was no fire. It could be a combination of incidents expressed as a burning building. Sometimes he thinks he spent much of forever as an idiot. Then he forgives himself. He must have been illiterate for most of history, like most everyone else. If he wanted to receive a formal education, he would have always been too old to blend in at a school. He must have educated himself through exposure, observations repeated over millennia, so that even if he wasn't naturally bright, which he suspects was the case, he eventually arrived at a learned place. The passages in the composition book are short, combining the transient nature of memory with his desire to keep moving and avoid detection. "Buenos Aires, 1741: Busy. Working docks. Some friends. Not too close." "Sao Paulo, 1759: Humid. Fell in love a little bit. Not too long." "Caracas, 1784: Like Buenos Aires." The entries do little more than mark time, as though immortality was the only thing he had going for him. Maybe he couldn't remember much from the pages that were lost in whatever the fire was. With paper scarce when he first started writing, and mobility as his guiding principle, he understands why his early diary was light. But the passages dated after he bought the composition book don't carry much more heft. The cover of the book commemorates New Mexico statehood. He had made it to the United States by then. He had forgotten how to speak Spanish and Portuguese. So much forgotten. So many events and people. Who was the person he fell in love with in Sao Paulo? There must have been others. None of them serious, at least not for the last thousand years. He would realize within his first lifetime or two that commitment was a bad idea as he outlived his love, or abandoned them before it reached that point in order to keep his secret. Fear of discovery is the only feature of his life that follows him across time. He wonders where the fear started, if he was scorned, banished or burned by superstitious people. He wonders if he was the inspiration for any of the characters in the Bible who live to age nine hundred. Eventually he came to fear any sort of attention. Even the thought of being admired or worshipped worries him. People would react to him in different ways, and there would be nothing he could do to control their reactions.

"I wish I was a musician," I said to Libby as I lined up my next shot after successfully completing the conquistador pose the following day. "You're only asking for a few minutes of someone's time to listen to your song. With a book, you're asking for a few days. Maybe several hours if they're really into it."

"How long is it?" she manned her post in the doorway. Too cold in the garage.

"On the short end," I got into character. "Like a really long short story. More of a novella than a novel."

"Then maybe you can't blame the length for lack of interest."

"Thanks, Libby."

I fell into an extra doleful stare and snapped the picture.

"Where are you supposed to be with that costume?" she gestured at my tunic.

"Just working on the docks," I shrugged. "Or a farm."

"Most of your outfits look the same."

"Yeah. I should add more props. Maybe even wear the exact same thing, but hold a shovel full of manure in one shot, be covered in flour in another."

"Why flour?"

"From working in a mill."

Libby sighed.

"Doesn't this guy ever have brushes with history? I thought maybe the conquistador phase was a turning point. That he was going to hang out with some famous explorer."

"It's more of a departure," I reviewed the costume rack looking to accessorize. "He's not really interested in exploring the New World. He just needs to hitch a ride from the old one. He deserts once they hit land. Doffs his helmet and armor and blends in with the stevedores. At least that's how he imagines it happened."

"Why would he have to imagine what happened in his own life?"

"He can't remember that far back."

"I guess that makes sense. I can't even remember last week."

I was about to speak, but she cut me off.

"No dementia jokes. I'm not there and it's too close to home."

"I would never," I deadpanned, both of us knowing I already had. "Especially when you're helping me make my point."

"He should have written things down."

"He wasn't able to record anything until there was access to paper, and even when there was, the pages would disintegrate over time."

"What does he imagine happened in the Old World?"

"Nothing."

"Why does he need to leave it?"

"Europe and Asia were growing more industrialized. It was getting harder to keep history at a distance."

"So he deliberately avoids any action," Libby realized.

"Yes."

"And you wonder why it's not selling."

I stopped drifting along the rack and stood my ground.

"Everyone always assumes that if they lived in the past, they would be right in the thick of history. Millions of square miles, millions of people, but of course they would just happen to be riding an elephant through the Alps with Hannibal, or waving a palm frond at Jesus. Nobody admits life would be a lot of days to fill, and we wouldn't know about any history being made around us. Even if news didn't travel so slowly, we'd be too busy trying to survive. I thought it would be funny to think of it that way. An ordinary person who lives forever."

"They're not ordinary if they can live forever."

"But he has to pretend to be."

"Why?" Libby was incredulous.

"Can you imagine what would happen if he was discovered?"

"He would be the most famous person in the world."

"Yes, and...?"

"He would make a lot of money on the public speaking circuit."

"Ah, Libby," I shook my head and turned back to the rack. "For someone who ran a theatre company, you sure suffer from a lack of imagination."

"I was on the Board," she reminded me. "My real job was managing a bank."

"Real job," I muttered loud enough for her to hear.

"Dreams don't pay."

"Somebody invented the bank. That was their dream."

"There you go," she wagged a finger at me, though it may have been wiggling naturally. "You could have your hero invent things with all his knowledge."

"He doesn't go back in time. He lives through it, constantly. He doesn't know the future."

"I know that. But he's lived so long."

"Memories, Libby. We talked about that. There's a limited supply. Part of his ordinariness is having an ordinary mind. Complete with average intelligence, mediocre problem-solving abilities, limited imagination, and of course, a typically sketchy memory."

"Change him."

"The book has already been written."

"It's not on paper."

"You're not getting it."

"Neither is anybody else."

I couldn't help but laugh. At times I wondered if she only hired me to sharpen her zingers.

"I'll admit," I picked out a fake leather vest and put it on over the tunic. "It may be one of those ideas that sounded better than it turned out to be. But it was fun to write, and it didn't cost me anything except some time. Plus it inspired this hilarious photo shoot."

I started to set up my next shot.

"What's he afraid of?" she asked.

"You could read the book."

"I'm just curious."

"You're really determined not to read it."

"Is he afraid they'll poke and prod him? Take his blood or something?"

"Now you're thinking," I complimented her as I switched the wallpaper swatch from a simulated wood to a light gray designed to imitate an overcast day.

"He doesn't want to be the subject of some horrifying experiments," she turned her questions into statements. "Especially if he's discovered in the days before modern medicine."

"That's definitely part of it," I said as I struck my standard pose. "But most of all..."

I took the photo then turned to face her.

"He doesn't want to mean anything to anyone."

She nodded and didn't seem able to stop. I was afraid I had tapped into a painful reflex and was about to apologize until she finally held still.

"Immortality is far-fetched enough," she said. "You should give him a superhuman memory. Just one more power."

"Is it really a power?"

I kept sounding so grave. I had Libby nodding again. I questioned whether my story also reflected something unnerving rather than funny and I was too involved in my own taste to notice. Maybe I did need to give it another look. In the meantime, I could lighten our conversation.

"I guess that's why people go with a time machine if they want to tell a story about connecting with the past," I said.

She smiled, much to my relief, and even played along.

"How come when someone does have a time machine," she said, "it doesn't matter where they are when they use it. All they have to do is put in the right date, and bam! There they are, setting sail with the Spanish Armada, even though they pressed the button in Kansas City."

"Artists just aren't practical," I indulged her.

•••

The immortal stays away from the East Coast when he crosses into the United States. More history is made there, the kind that makes it into more books. If he is caught living forever out west, news of him will become rumor by the time it reaches those with reach. His entries check in from places like Las Cruces, Durango, Flagstaff, Needles. As the twentieth century moves from horses to highways and the coasts tighten, he gravitates to larger cities so that he may blend in. First stop, Los Angeles, but it's not dense enough and generates too much news, so he migrates north to Fresno, then Sacramento, and finally Portland. He keeps his diary bland, and looks for stories in his scars. The one on the inside of his arm along the elbow has stitch marks. That must have left more than a physical mark, but nonetheless lies beyond his memory, so he estimates it happened in the 19th century, before the wide use of anesthesia. Maybe they poured alcohol onto the cut, or poured alcohol into him, enough so that he would black out. Whoever they were. Some of the scars that have faded look like they were rather grotesque when they were younger. There's a wide one running along the side of his leg below the knee that is by now level with the surface of the surrounding skin, but must have risen above it for years, maybe decades. He would have to stay off it and keep his leg raised for days, maybe weeks. If it happened while he was part of a nomadic tribe, if it took place that far back, they would have to leave him behind. He has always assumed he resisted civilization as long as he could, and stuck with the hunter-gatherers until there were no more of them to join. The scar is nothing but a different color nowadays. His healing powers are so remarkable that he wonders if he's died before, if his immortality involves not just avoiding death, but defying it. He gets sick. He's not immune. He wears dentures. If he survived all those tooth infections, maybe he is indestructible. Visits to the emergency room have made for some anxious moments, wondering if the tests are going to reveal him.

They never have. Everything is normal, they tell him. He even had a full-body scan after a workplace incident involving a wheelbarrow filled with limestone pavers and a wooden ramp suspended over a trench. He had always wanted a scan, out of curiosity, but with no Social Security number he never had insurance. Perhaps out of compassion, perhaps to avoid a lawsuit, the landscape architect who hired him paid for the appointment. As he slid slowly on his back into the whirring of the apparatus, he wondered if subconsciously he compromised the board over the trench on purpose in order to see if this machine would solve the mystery. But the tumble could have been lethal, and he doesn't want to die without answers, in case there are none afterwards. So he waits. At one point in the composition book he addresses himself directly. It is the only time he does this. After noting that he has moved to Fresno in 1972, he writes some time later, "I cannot tell you anything you do not already know. You have lived longer than I have." He does not include a date.

I posted my photo series on a variety of platforms and a fair number of people tagged it, liked it, noted it, and made some witty, mostly goofy comments about it, but seldom followed the link to my book. The downloads continued to be sparse, but nearly a year after I first published it, someone finally posted a review.

A person with the account name of "Ex Parson Brown" gave it five stars, and raved that "*The Logistics of Immortality* has more to say about the human condition than most of the ponderous non-fiction that professes to define a life well-lived. Beneath the surface of a clever romp through the fog of unrecorded history lies a profound meditation on the beauty of a finite lifespan. It's philosophy disguised as fiction, but the lessons don't generate any drag on the story. The author lets the events speak for themselves, and I can't speak highly enough about what he has created. Please read this book, and contact me with your thoughts about it. I would love to start a discussion group."

The person included an email contact that further riffed on the "Winter Wonderland" lyrics that inspired the Parson Brown account name: "iamnotasnowman".

I read the review aloud to Libby and she said we'd celebrate with a three-bean casserole.

"That's what you'd be making tonight anyway," I reminded her.

"I'll use a fourth bean. Any requests?"

"Black?"

"I'll see if I have any in the pantry."

"Thanks for asking."

While she prepared dinner, never mentioning whether or not she found black beans on her shelves, I debated whether or not to contact Ex Parson Brown to thank him or her for the kind words. The review had only been posted the day before, so I wondered if it was too soon.

I didn't want to come across as though I was religiously monitoring my site.

I was.

I just didn't want to come across that way.

Proof of someone paying attention made me think that maybe others were as well. I kept an even closer lookout to see if the rush was finally arriving, knowing it was foolish to believe, but not caring because it was fun to have hope.

Enough fun that I overcame my concern with appearances and sent Ex Parson Brown an email at the iamnotasnowman address. I introduced myself and thanked the person for the compliment. Tempted to ask if anyone had taken them up on their idea to form a discussion group, I instead acknowledged their clever account name and asked if they really were a lapsed member of the clergy, or simply a fan of Christmas music.

He wrote back within hours. He was a he, a he who was not worried about how far apart the timestamps were on his communications.

Hello Luca—

He said Hello instead of Dear...

So glad to hear from you. I was hoping my review would lure you into a correspondence. Your book really does mean a lot to me. You see, to answer your question, I am a somewhat lapsed clergyman. You were probably just joking by asking, a glib couple of lines to sign off gracefully, but it's true. I am a fan of Christmas music, too, but more to the point: I am a pastor who no longer believes in God. I still run a church. I'm no quitter. However, my motivation is to help people, not spread the Word. How fitting that my name is Pastor Lee. It sounds like an adverb, "pastorly", rather than a noun. I may not truly be a pastor any longer, but I am behaving pastorly. I won't saddle you with too many details of how the sun set on my faith. We only just met. I will say your book resonated with me for some very specific, personal reasons related to that subject. I've been searching the web with various combinations of the key words "everlasting" and "life", such was the initial source of my deprogramming. I couldn't help but wonder what we would do with such a thing as eternal life. Who would spend it with us? I'd love to have my grandmother with me as I remember her, but would she be willing to spend her eternal life as an old woman? Probably not. So who is this person in my paradise? A projection? A substitute version of some sort? And am I in her paradise as the child she recalls? If so, am I able to be everywhere at once? Attend each paradise I'm a part of? Or is it one at a time? Or one? At first I approached my mentors and colleagues with these questions, or at least those amongst them who like questions, but received the answer I was afraid of, variations on God Works In Mysterious Ways. Early in my education, I suspected if I was to suffer a crisis of belief, it would be thanks to that position, that fallback, that default: We can never really know. I have no problem with not knowing. I do have a problem with pretending to know. On my good days, I feel less like a liar and more like a benevolent fraud. Come on in, ye lost and searching. We have answers. Up to a point.

Sorry. I've said too much for a first email. You send me a thank you note, I send you a confession. I'll understand if I never hear from you again. If that be the case, I promise not to pester you with any more messages. Like I said, your take on the drawbacks of never-ending life truly struck a chord. Forgive me if I strum that chord too loudly, but I rarely get the chance to talk about it, given my work space and the degree to which it bleeds into my personal space. There's a lot that surrounds every Sunday, parishioners who want me to deliver the goods on God. Our church membership skews quite elderly. All those allusions to flocks and shepherds in the Bible truly reverberate when I look up and see all those white fleeces in the pews. We had a month recently wherein I visited so many care facilities and grieving households, I was convinced the average age of our congregation rose to "Officially Pronounced Dead". Those are obviously not the times to confide in anyone my views on God, and those times are frequent these days. Thank you for reading. This email is nearly

*as long as your book. At the risk of signing off in fawning fashion, may
I also say I like your name (in case I never hear back from you). Like
"Lucas", a name most would be more familiar with, but without the "s" at
the end, as if it doesn't quite reach its conclusion. One can either see it as
ending too abruptly, or not at all.*

Sincerely,

Pastor Lee

Since he wasted no time in replying, I went ahead and wrote him
back on the spot.

Hello Pastor Lee—

I also followed his lead on the friendly (Hello), less formal (Dear)
greeting style.

*I take it your invitation to start a discussion group has not generated
much interest. Such is the way of the web. It provides us with the chance
to share, and once we do, learn how few people care. I never suspected
just how exhilarating it would be to discover that someone does care,
that someone read what you had to say, had an emotional reaction to
it, thought about it, then sorted their thoughts into a logical response.
Mission accomplished, as far as I'm concerned. To receive that kind of
interaction even one time is worth it. Maybe more worth it than having
legions of fans, for I imagine the connections must be harder to make and
maintain in that case. In other words, don't hesitate in sharing anything
else that may be on your mind. Let the details of your conversion from
pastor to pastorly flow. I've got time to read. I work in elder care, so there
are long periods of space to fill. It's like being a border patrol agent or
Fish and Game warden: short bursts of action surrounded by lengthy
stretches of hard-fought boredom. Only instead of coyotes and poachers,
the action consists of incontinence and pill cutting. Looking forward to
learning more. Keep fighting the good fight, even as you find yourself under
new management.*

—Luca

•••

The immortal wonders if there are others like him. If he would know one if he met one. If there would be some kind of energy between them. That they would both somehow know. He suspects he's had children, if for no other reason than to see if they turned out like him. Unless he was honest with the mother about his condition, which he doubts he would be, he would have to disappear and come back to check on the child when he or she was grown. Study them from a distance for signs of aging as they touched the stage he is stuck on. Thirtysomething? Fortysomething? He probably did this multiple times to make sure, like parents who keep trying for a boy or a girl. The process took over a hundred years as he waited decades each until they passed the threshold. If it had worked, he would have kept having kids and built a family, a community of unique people who understood each other. They would support one another. Some would be angry at him for bringing them into a world they could never leave, but it would be easier as they grew in numbers, as enough offspring inherited whatever it is that makes them immortal to a point where it felt safe to live in the open. He believes such a community is the only way a woman like him could survive, if people like him are capable of being killed, are able to pass the test he's afraid to take. Avoiding discovery would be even more important for her. The backlash to a female immortal would be more vicious than the reception he has forever dreaded. He thinks of all the time he has spent by himself, avoiding contact, blending, disappearing, moving on, and how much more challenging it would be for a lone woman to dodge unwanted attention for thousands of years from people who held antiquated views of women back when those ideas were fresh. He imagines the unwanted results of that unwanted attention, the suspicion she would elicit, the leering and resentment, and the cruelty that would follow. She is trapped in a loop of superstition, stuck between the supernatural and the traditional, between witch hunts and male scrutiny. She has to keep moving, cannot stop for any extended period of time. She is okay from the late-twentieth century onward, if she can find her way to the right places, but getting there leaves her in tatters. The horrors stack up higher than she can reach, higher than history is long. If the immortal has encountered a woman like him, she was probably slumped in a doorway wrapped in filthy sleeping bags and quilts, whispering about torches and dogs and rotten breath. If there are others like him, none of them managed to create anyone in their image, either. There is no league of immortals. So he walks past her, wondering what the nonsense she murmurs could possibly mean.

•••

You should come visit.

Pastor Lee suggested after weeks of corresponding.

In checking our email threads, I noticed I have mentioned that my church is in a rather wealthy enclave, but I have yet to note the demographics. It is a resort area populated by many retirees who cashed in on their homes in bigger, even wealthier metro areas and moved to wine country. (We have lots of craft breweries, too; a desirable retirement destination must have fashionable alcohol on site so you can hide your drinking problem behind helping the local economy.) The reason I bring this up in greater detail is because I have someone from our congregation I'd like you to meet, someone who may be able to publish your book in more mainstream fashion: a broader online platform, hardbound and paperback copies with wide distribution, a promotional campaign, and the possibility of representation by a public speaking agency, depending on the demand.

Her name is Devon, and she made a fortune in the self-help industry before retiring to our little slice of heaven. I suggested she read your book, and in the process of discussing it with her, I mentioned our correspondences and how refreshing they have been. The combination of your writing and your engagement has her thinking we could be on to something special. I don't know how feasible it is for you to take time off, but if you can swing a couple of days, we'll spring for your airfare, and she has plenty of room at her estate. Please don't be shy about accepting our invitation. We wouldn't be extending it if we didn't think we'd be getting something out of it as well, to be honest. And if we're really being honest, I should go ahead and admit that while I keep using the "we" pronoun, she's the one paying for everything. I'm just the middle man. Story of my life. If not under God, then under Devon.

Let me know if this trip is at all possible, and if there are any logistical roadblocks we can help clear. Even if your visit doesn't result in an agreement, you get to spend some time in our perpetual Spring Break for old people.

Looking forward to your reply, and hopefully your presence.

Libby wasn't happy on the morning I left. She was okay with my trip at first, but grew steadily more grumpy after she found out who was going to fill in for me while I was away.

"There's a reason that woman is a sub," she complained. "Nobody can stand her voice for more than day. She talks baby talk, like she's addressing a toddler. Or a pet bird."

"Better than a crabby one," I tried to turn her to the bright side. "The agency has plenty of those."

"I didn't say she wasn't crabby. Plus she's so convinced of her own sweetness that she gets all puppy-eyed if you can't take it anymore and tell her so."

"I can ask for someone else."

"No," she waved me off with a sigh. "If she was the best available, I can only imagine how lousy the others would be. I used to think you didn't work through the agency because you wanted to be paid under the table. Then I realized they probably wouldn't take you. You're not their type. Oh well. It's not for long."

As the sub and I exchanged notes and pleasantries before I took off, I took note of her tonal syrup. Libby had a point. That voice needed salt. As we concluded the transition and she headed for Libby teeth-first, I offered facial condolences behind her back much to Libby's delight.

Most of the trip consisted of a layover at San Francisco International. People looked into their phones while they sat in the terminal. Some may have been reading. Most appeared to be watching something. The occasional person read a paperback. Relentless competition for everyone's time, options multiplying by the second, and someone thought my work could steal some of that time. I tempered my expectations so much that it didn't feel as though I was actually going anywhere. I was just sitting in a big airport, on my way to a small airport, and someone was going to pick me up and drive me around some pretty countryside and bring me to another person and we were going to talk about something I had done. I wasn't traveling, I was drifting.

I had searched Pastor Lee online and found some pictures of him, so I thought I knew what he looked like, but the photos I had seen turned out to be from his younger days. He recognized me from my "Ho-Hum Through the Ages" photo set, and spotted me first.

"You look just like your pictures," he approached me with arms outstretched.

"Hopefully not my expression," I accommodated his hug request.

"And I look older in person," he said as we detached.

"Well…"

He laughed at my hesitation.

"I'm more of an observer of the web, not a participant," he explained and led the way to his car.

We were due at Devon's first thing. Her estate was in the country, well outside the city limits, so if our drive was the only basis, it would seem that even a small airport in the region was unnecessary. We passed no more than a half-dozen homes in half an hour, each one atop its own hill that rose above the vineyards and fields where cattle grazed.

Our conversation centered on the small talk of travel, the flight quality and if everything went according to schedule. He allowed me to look out the window undisturbed every so often for a minute, taking in the green rows of grapes that climbed the golden hills in clear lines that blurred when they dipped onto flat land.

"I cannot tell you anything you do not already know," Lee said to break up the latest silent interlude. "You have lived longer than I have."

I needed a moment to adjust my focus from the scenery to the dialogue. I didn't even try to reply.

"That's the line that hooked me," he explained.

"You never mentioned that before."

"I didn't realize it until I read your book again to prepare for your visit."

"Lee," I settled back into a conversational angle. "You don't need to flatter me anymore. I'm happy to be here."

"I'm just continuing our discussion. Only now it's in person."

"Another level of weirdness for me," I apologized. "It was surprising enough to get a written reaction."

"That's the mark of a great piece of art," Lee ignored my contrition. "Every time you see it, or read it, or listen to it, you get something different from it. I suspect those words rang with me the first time, but I was too overwhelmed with the whole piece for any one part to sink in."

"What do you like about that line?" I decided to get in the habit of asking questions, as I suspected I would have a lot more in the coming days.

"It's the kind of thing Jesus would say to someone to make them feel as though they already knew what to do, and he was simply there to remind them. Like something I should say to the people in my church, and not even figuratively. They are all literally older than me."

"You weren't kidding when you said your membership is old."

He gave me a sidelong glance for as long as it was safe, which was pretty long since we were on a country road and there were no other vehicles around.

"If this deal with Devon works out," he finally looked ahead, "I'll post a more recent photo."

I laughed briefly, and speculated slightly longer as to what he meant by that, what sort of role he imagined himself playing in whatever they had planned.

The immortal studies history because he wants to see if any moments trigger any memories. Maybe he wasn't always far away from the action. He may have witnessed some occasions that stood the test of time with more notoriety than he has. He may have even participated in some historical event, if only by accident. In struggling to avoid contact, he could not have succeeded all the time, especially considering all the time he has had to fail. He hopes he has failed, that history caught up with him now and then. Unlimited life has left him with no life. But whenever he considers stepping into the light, he stands in line at a grocery store or eats at a fast food restaurant or sits on a bench at a county fair and looks at the people, and imagines all of them knowing who he is and wanting something from him, coming at him in waves with cell phones and voices raised, seeking a selfie with immortality. Or, for someone with an even lonelier life than the immortal, seeking the notoriety that would come with ending the world's longest streak. Whether that streak is a winning or losing streak is a question upon which the immortal wavers. So he keeps quiet and keeps reading books and articles, watching videos and documentaries, and wishes for a hook, a connection to the past he's perceiving. He especially likes re-creations: animations of the pyramids being built, digital simulations of a Roman Circus, actor portrayals of the Norman conquest, anything that took place before his journal entries started and revealed someone so committed to invisibility. Maybe he wasn't as cautious in his younger years, when he had yet to reach his first millennium. Though he suspects he was already thousands of years old by the time history started to be recorded, which would mean he arrived at that point with his paranoia fully developed and finely-tuned. When his latest passion for a specific historical era fades without a glimmer of recognition, he focuses on the advantages of immortality. As edgy as he may be about recognition, an endless life has provided him with a certain serenity, an acute awareness that today's troubles will pass. He's a living testament to expressions like "Time heals all wounds" and "Life goes on." And on and on and on. "This too shall pass." Except for him. A party that never ends isn't really a party. He has visceral reactions to seeing death portrayed, whether on film or in writing. He wonders if the jolt he experiences while studying death indicates the kind of connection he has failed to discover in history. Maybe he has gone through the act of dying without its most common side effect. Or he may be jealous. He doesn't dream of death, or have visions of it, or fear it. His body and mind are way past those worries. He finds it hard to believe he hasn't experienced some kind of accident given his bottomless opportunities, which doesn't make him any more inclined to rig another one, to put himself in danger on purpose. Not without proof. Not without confirmation.

•••

"Here we are," Pastor Lee announced as we straightened out of a lengthy curve in the paved road and veered off onto a gravel one. "Devon's Gate."

I expected something more ornate.

It was the kind of gate used to keep cows in, rather than people out. No security system, no keypad or cameras, no lock, just a chain with a hook keeping it from swinging open, and wooden posts on each side with barbed wire fanning out from them.

Lee asked if I would mind "doing the honors."

I hopped out and unhooked the chain, which slithered down a metal rung of the gate with a series of clacks, one for each link, until it hung from its post.

Lee drove slowly past to keep the dust down. We waved at each other. I closed the gate and wrapped the chain into place.

"Why did we wave at each other?" I asked once I was back in the passenger seat.

"You started it."

"I thought we did it at the same time."

"It was close. Maybe I was thanking you for holding it open."

"And I was thanking you for not kicking up the dust."

"We're nice people."

"We certainly are, Reverend."

We drove for maybe a mile, which took maybe five minutes. We drove at a crawl, so it was difficult to gauge distance and time. The land was untouched, aside from the road we rolled along. The grass held its green in the fading wake of winter rains that had passed weeks before. Rallies of wild mustard and purple lupine flared between isolated old oak trees that appeared to contort their thick trunks and flex their leafless branches and stretch their mossy shoots in an effort to draw attention to themselves. Lee guided the vehicle over some rises and through some dips. By the third rise, the house was visible, spread across the highest ground we had encountered. It was impressive, but out of place, like the centerpiece of an urban redevelopment project marked by glass, polished metal, and think wooden beams.

"Not exactly what you'd call a ranch house," Lee read my reaction.

"Did she build it?"

He nodded.

"It's more corporate headquarters than dream home. Her husband died right before construction, and she completely changed the plans."

The hill was high enough that the road needed to be carved into it and twist a few times to reach the paved plot that spread out from the foundation of the house. Lee parked in no particular space and jumped out to lead the way, knocking at the same time he opened the door.

"Hello?" he called to no response. "Devon?"

The house looked even larger on the inside. A high ceiling in the main room pushed the second story to the edges behind a balcony corridor that lined three sides of the cavernous silo, with a massive window taking up the fourth wall.

Lee called her name one more time, and the echo reproduced two more versions.

We heard her coming before she said anything, the sound of her footsteps rising and ricocheting between doorways. She materialized cradling a model monster truck with a remote control tucked under one arm.

"Hello Pastor Lee," she said as though passing him in the street.

And pass him she did, even as he spread his arms for a hug in what I was gathering to be his customary greeting.

"Can I give you a hand with that?" he kept his arms open but raised his palms as a symbol of the help he was willing to give.

"No, no," she insisted. "I can manage."

I saw no reason to doubt her. She was a very spry version of old age, ruffled skin but taut muscles, gray hair but a thick crop of it. She headed toward the doors in the wall of windows.

"This is Luca," Lee tried to flag her down.

"Of course it is," she didn't break stride.

Lee shot me a shrug. We followed her outside.

The backyard was a gateway to the rest of the property. The tiled area was large enough to hold a set of patio furniture and a grill, but gave way shortly to a lightly manicured swath of land featuring some redwood chip paths and half-wine barrels with annuals planted in them, which in turn gave way to a grove of oak trees that gathered at the lip of the hill.

Devon walked to the edge of the tiles facing the open space. She placed the mini monster truck upside down on the ground, then used the remote to engage the motor. The wheels started to spin fast enough to shake the truck. It wobbled like a turtle flipped over onto its shell trying to get back on its feet. The motor hummed a low note while the tires spun a high note. As I considered turning to Lee to see if he had any idea what she was doing, two longhorn cattle climbed into view, stepping onto the top of the hill and into the oak grove.

Each had different markings, one brown with white speckles, the other mostly gray. Both had massive horns that seemed long enough to protrude from a triceratops back when the herbivores that grazed the land were cold-blooded. The longhorns stopped short of the manicured area and stared at the upturned remote control monster truck. Three more rose from the horizon behind them and joined the inspection, then two more, and finally a wave of horns crested over the top, jostling for position to witness the source of the noise that lured them into the grove. They held their ground a bean bag's toss away from the overturned vehicle and started to moo.

When their voices exceeded the drone of the spinning wheels, Devon cut the engine, dropped the remote, and strode forward to greet them. She rubbed the snout of the first one who had made it up the hill, the brown heifer with the white speckles, then turned to face us amid the chorus of moos.

"I saw you coming up the drive and decided to make an impression."

"Why have I not seen this before?" Lee asked above the din.

"No need to impress you."

"See how much she liked your book?" he lightly tapped my forearm.

"Not so fast, Lee," she grabbed one of the horns that sloped above the long brown head, then clutched a horn of the gray one to her other side.

"How do you get them to stay out of the yard?" I asked.

"Invisible fence," she jostled the horns which shook both heads.

"But they're not wearing shock collars," I noted.

"They don't need to anymore," she let go of them with a kiss on each forehead and walked toward us.

"Hello, Luca," she extended her hand.

"Devon," I nodded as I shook it.

"What is your book about?"

I looked at Lee.

"I read it," she assured me.

"Are you going to offer us anything to drink or eat?" Lee asked.

"We'll get there," she waved him off. "I had longhorns to serenade."

The livestock had stopped voicing their concern over the remote control and were milling about, the grass and leaves crunching under their feet, their collective breaths and occasional snort sounding like a pod of whales.

I chose my words.

"It's about someone who leads a not-very-interesting life that never ends."

She smiled.

"Why?"

"It's supposed to be funny."

"Life?"

"Just the book."

"If you had to come up with a moral of the story…"

"It sucks to be immortal."

"So where does that leave the rest of us?" she crossed her arms. "Should we live like there's no tomorrow? Live like we're dying?"

"Not necessarily," I addressed the arm cross.

"My husband died thanks to that You-Only-Live-Once shit. Extreme skiing. Dropped from a helicopter on top of a mountain and hit a tree on the way down. Falling down, mind you. Wasn't even on his skis. What an inspiration. People said that during the funeral. To my face. How inspiring they found his zest for life. How he died doing something he loved. Indeed. Who doesn't love plummeting over rocks and snow to their death, breaking bones and dislocating joints along the way. His last words were surely some form of blood-curdling scream, if he could manage to make any noise at all. The tree was probably for the best. I shudder to think of the condition he would be in if he survived. I have some aggressive local beer and homemade chile relleno. Does that sound good?"

She smirked at Lee.

"Great," he pulled himself out of her story and into the moment. "Anything I can do to help?"

"No," she retrieved her remote control monster truck and the longhorns appeared hopeful that she'd spin the wheels again.

"Have a seat, make yourself comfortable," she said as she passed us on her way back to the house, to the disappointment of the herd.

Lee and I obliged. We lowered ourselves into chairs around the table, each of us exhaling on our way down. When we were out of breath, he looked over at me and asked "Well?"

I looked over at the livestock who continued to lurk and size us up, wondering if we had any vehicles to overturn.

"This trip is already worth it. Whatever else happens is gravy."

I bowed my head toward the huddle of horns.

"Sorry," I said to them. "I meant to say 'icing on the cake.'"

"That's sweet of you," Lee chuckled. "But nobody's eating those cattle. Purely ornamental. They're a collection, not a herd."

I looked at them and felt grateful for their sake, then looked across the rest of the landscape and felt grateful for everything.

"Live slowly," he said after some silence, as though narrating my appreciative gaze along the horizon.

I agreed with a languid series of nods while keeping my sights on the doughy hills dotted with oaks.

"That's the pitch she has in mind," he clarified.

I turned my attention from across the terrain to across the table.

"Her pitch to me?" I asked.

"To the public."

"So we're doing this?"

"It's only a matter of marketing now."

"Wow," I looked out at the countryside again, but didn't really see it this time.

"You've never struck me as the kind of person who says 'wow.'"

"It has been a while."

He let me wade through the eddy of information and emotion until Devon returned holding a metal bucket of beer bottles on ice in one hand, a platter of chile rellenos with plates under it in the other, and silverware and napkins pinned to her side by her elbow.

"You really don't think the immortal could be a woman," she said as she laid out the items.

"What kind of beer is that?" Lee again tried to slow her down.

"An IPA with one of those ridiculous names that plays off the word 'hop'. Hippity Hop, Hop on Pop, some joke that dies on the label. Stop cutting in, Lee. The man can handle himself."

"I considered making the character a woman," I wanted to prove her correct about me and wrong about my book. "I really did. But most of human history dictated that decision."

"There are parts of the world with a less discouraging record of patriarchy. Your story leans rather far to the West."

"It's what my audience would be familiar with, when I dared imagine having an audience. I tried to portray him as being very self-aware when it comes to his place in the world. His location, not just his situation. There's that passage where he wonders how far and in how many directions he's traveled, but suspects he avoided places where he would look different than the general population, since he prefers not to stand out."

"Poor guy," Devon finished setting the table and sat down. "He could have gone deep into a jungle somewhere and been worshipped, Heart of Darkness style."

"The jungle is full of things that feed his fear of death."

"An immortal who's afraid of dying," Lee celebrated as he served himself.

I bounced off his latest compliment into more evidence to address Devon's criticism.

"It's implied he may have hit the Silk Road," I reminded her. "All that trade meant a lot of intermingling, and a chance to go East. He feels a strong connection to the Indus Valley, thinks he may have migrated there for a spell. But yes, the West is the only portion he's able to recall. I had to take him there eventually for the reader's sake."

"Him," she scoffed. "You could have made her a skilled fighter. Maybe learned martial arts as part of her journey."

"That's not the kind of story I wanted to tell. The immortal doesn't fight other people. He fights the tedium and mistrust created by his bizarre genetics, which involves hardly speaking or interacting with people, which is a trait more commonly associated with men."

"Her fighting skills could be a metaphor."

"Those skills would have to be extraordinary to fend off that many attacks for that long, and like I said, this is not a superhero narrative, or action adventure. This is an everyday person with a crushing number of every days."

"But finding the beauty in it," Lee jumped in. "Longing for normalcy, appreciating the small moments because he can't reach for any large ones."

Devon uncapped a beer and took a swig. She glanced back and forth at the two of us.

"You can't resist, can you, Lee?" she smiled.

"Not when it comes to this, no."

He cut into the chile on his plate.

"And you really think it will matter that much to other people?"

"A thousand yesses," he wagged his fork with a portion of chile on the tip. "With a hundred exclamation marks after each yes."

I took advantage of their banter to grab a chile and beer of my own.

"Then I guess we need to get our messaging straight," she said.

"What's wrong with leaving it open to interpretation?" Lee lifted a bottle from the bucket and let it drip before setting it by his plate. "Imagine conversations like this one happening all over the place, leading up to a room full of them at a convention. We should encourage debate. How many movements leave themselves open to interpretation?"

The word 'movement' caught my attention, but I had just taken a bite.

"None of the successful ones," Devon said.

"That's why outsiders find them so creepy."

"Nobody found our seminars creepy, and they were very straightforward. People were free to follow our advice, or not. But there was no doubt as to what we were suggesting."

"Like you said, they were seminars. They weren't movements."

"There's that word again," I swallowed and cleared my throat. "I thought we were here to discuss publishing my book."

Devon and Lee exchanged a look.

"Sorry if we're getting a bit ahead of ourselves," Devon took the lead. "I've never been much of a Power Point and prospectus type when it comes to sales pitches. My husband and I put on a few presentations at some academic conferences back when we were still professors, and people just started inviting us to do more. I've never bid for anything."

"Bid?" I asked. "What is there to bid on? I figured we'd go with whatever the industry standard is for book royalties, with a finder's fee of some sort for Lee. What is this other thing? This movement?"

Devon enjoyed some of her own cooking before explaining.

"I've been in the Should Business a long time, Luca."

"The Should Business?"

"That's what I call the self-help industry. The business of telling people how they should live their life. If they want this, they should do that. If they want that, they should do this."

"Got it," I took another bite and sat back, proud of myself for dictating the pace of the conversation.

"It's never about the book," she continued. "The book is a calling card. It's a springboard into seminars, conferences, and residencies. Speaking engagements that pay way more than your book sales ever will."

"My book isn't self-help."

"Isn't it?" she probed, as though I was supposed to reconsider everything I had assumed about my own work.

I let an amount of time pass that I imagined would indicate I was in the process of having just such a revelation.

"No," I said instead.

Devon was undaunted by my skepticism.

"Why did you write it?" she asked.

"Like I said, to be funny."

"For whom?"

"Anyone who happens to read it."

"You want people you've never met before to think you're funny."

"I guess so, yes. That's the long version of what I said."

"You want to be admired."

"I don't know about that."

"What would you call it, then? This desire to be liked by strangers."

"I want my work to be admired. My work doesn't depend on people seeing me. My physical presence is not required for someone to enjoy it. Am I doing this right? Have I expressed the same thought in enough different versions?"

Devon smiled.

"Then why the photo shoot?" she asked.

Lee snickered.

"Sorry," he motioned my way. "I'm not saying she got you or anything. I'm just thinking of that picture with the ram horn."

"I like the floppy hat shot," Devon joined him. "Like one of those portraits of a Romantic poet, but with a tattered work shirt and dirty face, as if he stole the hat off the head of some fop walking by. Very clever commentary on social class."

"Those were taken to promote the book," I defended myself. "Not me."

Devon glanced at Lee as if waiting for a signal.

I buried myself in my food.

"Look," she used her tone of voice as a peace offering. "We can merely publish the book if that's what you want. It's fine. I didn't care for it as much as Lee, but then Lee cares for it in the true sense of the word. Cares for it like a child or pet. And I trust Lee has some pretty keen insights into the kind of people we can appeal to. People who know what to do, but need to hear it from someone else. Easy fixes. I'm too old for any other kind."

Her expression paved the way for a smile that didn't quite form, curbed by emotions she was not expecting. She covered them by concluding her plug.

"If you want to make a little extra money, go on a nine-city book tour, we'll make that happen. Or you can make a lot of money and build a legacy."

I took a sip from the bottle. It was good beer, but she was right, it was also rather bold. I was grateful for its bite. If it went down any easier, I would have gulped the entire contents in seconds while considering their offer.

She said I didn't need to decide at that moment. I still had another day to spend as their guest. There were wineries to visit, restaurants in town, conversations to have that didn't always revolve around my goofy little book.

They weren't making any guarantees, but they had a good feeling about me.

I had never heard that from anyone before. People said I was nice, or doing a good job, but nobody ever spoke of my potential. There was never a bright future.

We never got around to having one of those moments where we shook hands or raised our glasses in a toast. I never even said "yes", not definitively. Everything tasted so delicious. They simply started planning, and I started to contribute.

• • •

The immortal doesn't worry about telling anyone he's immortal. He's not in the habit of doing so, but slips on occasion. Maybe a hundred occasions, if he could remember them all, if his memory was as prodigious as his lifespan. The slips never matter. Nobody believes him. If anyone wanted to know the truth, they would have to know him longer than he allows anyone to know him. Nobody has ever told him "You haven't aged a bit." He has a recurring dream, though, that he dreams often enough to make him wonder if it's based on a true story. It takes place in a combination of languages that change with every replay. Some he used to speak, like Spanish and Portuguese, and he recognizes them whenever they are voiced. Others, like Greek and Armenian, he may have spoken before, but he has to look up whatever words he can remember from the latest version of the dream to find out where they came from. The dream in all of its forms takes place in no particular location, as far as he can see. No landmarks stand out. The scenes play out in nondescript rooms of tables and chairs, with windows that only reveal night or day. Both darkness and lightness have been the backdrop for what transpires between him and an antagonist he can never quite describe because the antagonist looks different in every draft. He approaches the immortal early in the dream and asks if he remembers him. The antagonist doesn't know that the immortal remembers very little because there is so much to remember. So no, the immortal says, in whatever languages are currently featured, sometimes all in the same sentence, one or two words per language at a time. No, he does not remember him. The antagonist presses him. "You don't remember a night twenty years ago when you got really drunk in that tavern with stuffed ravens hanging from the ceiling?" "You don't remember that day thirty years ago when you got into an argument during the construction of the temple gardens?" "You don't remember forty years ago when you were on the road in a convoy

38

that was held up and robbed?" No. The immortal never remembers whichever incident drives a particular reiteration of the dream. He doesn't recall his drunken confession of immortality, his bragging on the job site, his threat to the thieves. He certainly doesn't remember the antagonist being there when it happened. The antagonist was just a boy then, a boy too young to know that such things are impossible. He stalked the immortal while he still lived in the same town, then trailed him when he moved on, because the antagonist was old enough by then to strike out on his own. He doubted himself, debated giving up his pursuit. A lot of time passed and the immortal didn't appear to age, but maybe he was just healthy. The antagonist had come too far to surrender. He went back to his hometown to see if the people he had known looked palpably older. They did, especially compared to the immortal. He had his first sliver of evidence. He went back again and found some people who remembered the immortal. He didn't tell them why he was interested in their memories. When he builds his case high enough, he is ready for his obsession to pay off. He tells the immortal what he's been doing. The immortal asks why. The antagonist wants to know the secret to everlasting life. When the immortal tells him he doesn't know, that he was born this way, and that no mystical, magical figure has materialized to explain everything and mentor him, the antagonist does not take it well. He's wasted most of his childhood and all of his adulthood so far. He keeps asking him for an answer, so insistent there must be one that with each denial from the immortal, his rage grows to a level where he attacks, and the immortal kills him in self-defense. In that version. In an alternative ending, the antagonist decides that if he can't unlock the key to immortality, he can at least make some money off of it. So he bribes the immortal, threatening to out him unless he contributes to a hush fund. In this ending, it's the immortal whose rage escalates with each payment extorted from him. He kills the antagonist again, and still thinks of it as self-preservation. Regardless of motive, each ending is grisly. The dream takes place well before his current cache of memories was catalogued, centuries if not millennia, so when he uses a weapon to murder the antagonist, it's something crude: a rock, or staff, or dull blade. In most of the cuts, he uses his bare hands, which is the worst. He wakes in a spasm, shakes for however long it takes to get back to sleep, if he does at all, with an unsettling appreciation for why we invented more sophisticated weapons. He consults a variety of hypnotists to check if the dream is a product of any repressed memories. Some of the hypnosis is performed in the offices of psychiatric professionals with modern art on the walls next to their degrees, other sessions in tents or trailers set up at state and county fairs. None of the hypnotists have looked horrified upon snapping him out of his past. No murders are mentioned by the immortal while in a trance. Some hypnotists note references to past eras, detailed accounts of old machinery, ancient farming practices and construction techniques, even speaking in foreign languages. But they never suspect anything. The ones with doctorates behind them attribute his knowledge to the collective unconscious. The dusty mystics attribute it to reincarnation. None of them ever asks if he's immortal. If any ever do, he will say yes. The evidence takes more time to compile than any one person is willing to wait. Someone could take pictures of him, or videos, or he could take pictures of himself, and hold onto them. But photos and videos can be altered. Proof has to be in person. By holding still, by keeping in touch, the immortal is the only one who can prove he is immortal.

The book cover was peppered in rosy recommendations from people Devon knew from the Should Business. I knew what the blurbs were going to say because Lee wrote them and ran them by me for approval. He then sent the list to those who would be quoted so they could choose the words that would be put in their mouths. Dibs were dependent on Devon. The more she liked someone, the earlier they received the list, presenting them with more options for their attribution.

I was only familiar with one of the names, a pop therapist with a podcast who often appeared as a talking head in the split screens on cable news programs that Libby and some of my other patients liked to watch in the afternoon. Dr. Wanda specialized in finding different ways to say that we lived in a corrosive media landscape. She also claimed on the cover of *The Logistics of Immortality* that it was "an exciting new voice in a field that desperately needs more seeking and less preaching." I asked Lee how many options she had to choose from, and he said she was rather high on the list, having been a keynote speaker at a dozen of Devon's conventions. He thought she may have even read the advance copy of the book that was sent to everyone.

I initially didn't recognize the actor Devon stuck with to voice the audio version of the book, as he made his living primarily in voiceover work, including reading some of Devon's previous books aloud. Upon looking him up, I realized I had encountered some of his characters from the animated shows that grandkids of past clients had enjoyed. I remembered his turn as a talking goat who manages a frozen yogurt shop where the rainbow of flavors and toppings iron out their differences, and his role as a disaffected plastic straw who floats through the ocean menacing the sea life he encounters. I never did meet him, as he performed the book in a recording studio in Burbank.

I started to think of it as *the* book rather than *my* book, a feeling which grew more pronounced with each phase of the publishing process. By the time I saw it on a shelf, I felt as though I had also attached my name to something someone else had written. Each blurb was longer than my bio, which simply read that I grew up in foster care and now care for the elderly. When I first saw the galley proof, I asked Devon if we should include more about me and she asked what for. Unless there was an Ivy League doctorate in my past I had failed to mention, we were better off vague.

"You're not an authority on anything," she said. "You're not a clinical psychologist, a professor of philosophy. We need to promote you as a kind of mystic or medium."

She insisted I deactivate my photo series, and hoped that no one had any screenshots of it. The people we were trying to peg were not easily impressed.

The first bookstore reading was not far from Libby's house, so I took her along, but she was nowhere near the target audience. Phase one of the plan involved a book tour focusing on cities that attract ambitious people who want to believe they are no longer ambitious, places that are smaller than the places they left, but with all the amenities and plenty of opportunities to build it in their image. Places with bookstores. Devon and Pastor Lee wanted to aim for successful, talented people who were let down by their determination. Not because they fell short of their goals, but because they reached them, and found nothing there but the opportunity to brag about what they had accomplished, if they were prone to brag, which they were not. People who wanted a sense of the eternal, but had too many questions about religion. They needed to solve the mystery on their own, achieve spiritual fulfillment the same way they had achieved everything else, thanks to their initiative and drive.

"I was hoping to see Dr. Wanda," Libby said as she sat by my side in the first row of folding chairs facing a table stacked with copies of the book and a podium I would eventually occupy.

"I'm hoping to see anyone at this point," I answered as I surveyed the empty rows of white plastic chairs behind us.

Lee was on my other side.

"We don't need a large audience," he leaned into me and repeated something Devon often said. "We need a devoted one."

"And by one, you mean the number of people here," I quipped.

"Is there somebody here?" Libby slowly swiveled to look behind us.

I focused on what was in front of us and played off her joke with a hurt face. My performance started to become a lived reality when Lee, thankfully, interrupted its spread.

"There are plenty of people in the store," he said. "Lots of smart people roaming through the shelves that will be drawn in when they hear you."

My introduction was conducted by a young woman who acted as though she lost an argument with the other employees on who was going to be stuck with the chore. Using the book as her script, she read my bio, the summary, one of the blurbs, then ducked away. Lee and Libby clapped and hooted enthusiastically enough for a few shoppers on the periphery to stop their browsing and offer polite applause. I slouched to the stand and Lee started recording a video.

After a brief "thank you" and a long pause to resist the sarcasm I nearly flung at the empty introduction and matching chairs, I stuck to the pagination, reading the initial passages that provide some exposition, then jumped to a section in which the immortal plays a game familiar to many. We find ourselves in a mundane moment realizing we will not remember it, so we try to, even though there is no reason to. We don't need to recall the dirty toothbrush we saw on the sidewalk somewhere between the office and the bus stop on that day nothing happened at work, or that doodle we drew on the napkin while we ate lunch at the taqueria which isn't as good as the other one that was too crowded that afternoon. But we decide to try because no one else will. We have the most extensive record of our own existence, and we want to add to the archives. Or maybe it's to exert some control over our minds, which seem to have so much control over us. The immortal plays the game with no such motives. He knows the records will be lost, and control needs to be controlled. This may sound bleak, he thought so too at first, but surrendering has allowed him to play the game without any pressure. When he finds the napkin later on in his pocket and does not remember doodling on it, he is not alarmed. All he does is decide whether or not it's a good doodle. What he draws on a napkin carries the same dimensions as what he says to his boss. His walk to the bus stop is as lost on memory lane as a trip to his lover's hometown. Living ten thousand years or more will have that effect.

I read the passage in what I hoped was a light tone. I earned some laughs, not just from Lee, but from people who started to fill the seats at the ends of the rows. I would look up and see a square developing as the edges grew occupied and the center remained empty. I finished the reading to applause that was slightly louder and less polite than before, and felt better about bothering. Lee jumped up and asked if there were any questions, waving off the young employee who had been imposed upon to introduce me. The square dissipated, the people composing its sides fading back into the aisles from which they came.

"Well, if you're too shy to ask in front of everyone," Lee announced, "Luca will be hanging around for some one-on-one time if you'd prefer."

Most of the people continued to casually flee, some returning Lee's smile with a smile of their own and a nod. Libby glared back and forth at both ends of the exodus from her seat and shook her head. But one of them stayed behind, a woman who looked like she would spend time with her grown daughter and expect people to say they looked like sisters.

"Remember," Lee reminded me under his breath, "Ask questions, don't make statements."

I came out from behind the lectern to greet her.

"This isn't what I expected," she said.

"What were you expecting?" I asked.

"Your book doesn't seem to have any lists."

"Lists?"

"You know, ten habits of highly successful people, five ways to simplify your life. That sort of thing. I've come to expect it from Devon's imprint."

"You know Devon?"

"I've bought some books, attended a conference."

"You prefer lists?"

"They're straightforward, they get to the point. This seems like more of a novel, something that needs to be analyzed. I guess I shouldn't judge until I've read it. If I read it."

I saw Libby fidget in her chair and roll her eyes. I averted mine and refocused on our first prospective customer.

"You don't like analyzing things?" I asked.

"I'm a data analyst. I'm not sure I want to do it in my spare time."

"Especially something fictional," I commiserated.

"I'll read a story if I want to be entertained. If you're offering advice, just give it."

"Are you concerned you'll come to the wrong conclusion?"

"Maybe," she conceded.

"That's not a problem."

"So there's a really clear ending to your story. The message is blatantly obvious."

"It's mostly the immortal reminiscing about a life he can't remember much of."

"There's no plot," the woman held up her hand as though stopping me, even though I had already stopped.

"Not really."

"A self-help book with no lists, a novel with no story."

Lee started to chuckle off to the side. I looked over and saw that he had been recording the conversation.

The woman noticed too.

"I will not sign a waiver," she said.

"Strictly for research," Lee pledged. "It's early. We want to find ways to hone our message."

"What message?" she scoffed, and headed back into the books.

Lee and I looked at one another as if to see who would sigh or shrug first. Libby interrupted us.

"Would you sign my copy?" she raised a book between us.

It flapped in her vibrating hand like a flag in a stiff wind.

"I didn't know you had one," I smiled.

"I grabbed it from the table," she nodded at the stacks.

"Plenty to go around," I lamented.

"Would you mind buying it for me?" she lowered the copy as it seemed to put on weight in her rickety grip. "I didn't bring any money."

"Of course."

"I'll pay you back."

"It's on me."

"No, I insist. I really liked your reading, and now that it's a real book, I'm going to dive in."

"I appreciate that, Libby."

I took the book to the podium, grabbed a pen, and started scribbling.

Lee started recording the moment.

"Seriously?" I asked.

"Shhh," he hissed. "It's an action shot for the website, based on a perfectly legitimate autograph request."

"*Based on*..." I shook my head and finished with a flourish.

"But wait," Lee said. "There's more."

I looked up and another woman was clutching a copy of the book several arms' lengths away.

"Oh," I raised my eyebrows in tune with the heightened volume of my surprise. "Just a moment."

I handed Libby her freshly-signed copy. She pursed her lips and raised her eyebrows higher than mine, then reverted to a normal expression before she turned to pass the woman on her way back to the chair.

The woman in waiting stepped forward and apologized.

"For what?" I asked.

"Not sitting down in the designated area, not asking questions," she explained. "I got a little self-conscious when I saw the layout. I like to participate in discussions, but not start them."

"I'm the same way," I assured her.

Lee started recording again.

"Do you mind?" I asked her, not Lee.

"It's fine," she had sufficiently warmed up.

"Promotion," I muttered.

"I get it."

"What's your name?" I reached for her copy.

"Claire," she handed it to me.

I thanked her in writing for attending before signing off with a phrase Devon suggested: *You Already Know.*

"Already know what?" Claire read the inscription as I handed it back.

I stuck with the response Devon also suggested when someone inevitably asked.

"How to live a good life."

"I do?"

"It's only a matter of following through."

"Okay," she didn't seem convinced, but also seemed to figure there are worse things that could be said.

"We'll be holding some events this summer," Lee stopped recording and proclaimed. "Check our *Logistics of Immortality* website."

"I will," she smiled. "Thank you."

She strode back into the shelves.

Once she was out of sight, Lee raised his arms and stopped short of shouting "Whooo".

"That's almost condescending," I said. "You're not my Dad and I'm not playing in a youth soccer game."

"I'll get used to it," he said.

"We had one disgruntled customer and one satisfied."

"Don't I count?" Libby asked.

"In the grand scheme of things, yes..." I started to explain.

She indicated I needn't say anything more.

"I know we planned on relying heavily on word of mouth," Lee thought aloud. "But maybe we need to market more aggressively."

"You think?" I swept my hand across the valley of empty chairs.

"Devon's expecting some video. We'll see what she has to say after she's reviewed it."

"Including the testy one?"

"You mean the teachable moment?"

"Yes, Pastor. The learning experience."

"Ooh, I like that one, too," Lee cooed as he sent the files to Devon. "Such a quick study."

He tapped the screen one more time to complete the transaction before announcing "Let's eat."

"My treat," Libby rose from her chair.

"But it's mushroom quesadilla night," I tested her resolve.

"Damn all convention," she waved off years' worth of mushroom quesadillas.

"See?" Lee went over to her and lent his arm to lean on. "You're changing lives, Luca."

Libby realized she was out of the loop when it came to the restaurant scene, as her favorites had been surpassed and in many cases shut down, so she relied on us to compare Yelp searches and find a place suitable for celebration.

Devon called while we were splitting a crème brulee for dessert. The kitchen was closed and our table had a buffer zone of empties around us, so we decided we could safely face time without anyone finding us obnoxious. I scooted next to Lee as he propped the back of his phone against a water glass to frame us.

"The reading was good," she said after barely acknowledging our hellos. "Nice tone, Luca. Stick with that moving forward."

"Thank you, Devon. But…"

"Yes, about that feisty one."

"Sorry about that."

"What for?"

"I started to make statements, broke from the questions. Your directions worked so well when it came to that other woman, right down to her reaction to the signing and our exchange. I feel like if I had stuck to the plan with the other one it would have gone better."

"No," Devon insisted. "No. You took that as far as you could. I'm glad she happened, especially right away. Let her be a reminder of whom we're not interested in."

"Yup," Lee piped in, nodding his whole upper body.

"If they're not receptive within a couple of questions, bye," Devon waved. "Thank them for coming and move on."

"But we're trying to build an audience."

"Remember what we keep saying about our audience," Lee said.

"Devoted, not large," I recited.

"They don't want to be part of a crowd," Lee continued. "What we offer has to seem like an individual pursuit. That's the only way we can lure people out of their personal entertainment centers in their homes."

"They need to already be projecting a moral onto your story by the time they interact with you," Devon said. "They are peaceful searchers, dissatisfied but not angry. Consider that first woman. Is there anything we can possibly do for her? Anything any program can do? And when she emerges as the same bitter person she was before, will she be the least bit self-reflective? Or will she feel let down yet again and embrace the resentment she relies on for comfort? Naturally she will vent in public, on the web, with us as the focus of her latest vendetta. Then again, maybe she was just having a bad night. Regardless, they're out there. Lots of them, looking for an easy fix and coming down hard when you can't provide it. By exercising some discretion up front, we'll end up with a scroll of success stories longer than a red carpet. And to make that happen, we need people who don't need us. They only think they do."

"Your book is a Rorschach test," Lee said. "If they find a message in it, they're inches away from the answers they want, so whatever they find in our company will be brilliant, because it was based on their own ideas."

"Meanwhile," Devon sounded as though her finger was inching toward the red button, "in spite of my aversion at my age to large groups of people, we could obviously use a bigger turnout. I thought a departure from our usual product would generate some buzz, but our crowd apparently doesn't know what to make of it. I guess there's a fine line between different and weird. We spooked the herd. I'll weigh the options. Maybe order a buyback so we can climb some bestseller lists, astroturf some comments on the website, sick some bots on social media..."

"Reactivate the photo series..." I kicked in a joke.

"Speaking of bad ideas," she stepped on my gag. "No videos where it's you talking to the camera. None of that YouTube shit. We're trying to capture a smart group of professionals. Becoming an internet sensation kills any chance of that. Keep doing what you do, Luca, only less of it."

She hung up before I could respond.

Lee and I looked at each other. He blew a brief laugh through his nose. I went with my mouth.

"You're not going to be working for me much longer, are you?" Libby asked from across the table.

I glanced over at Lee, instinctively growing more dependent upon his public relations. He offered silence, a signal I was on my own.

"Probably not," I answered her.

Libby went slack and stared at the table.

"I'll stay as long as it takes to find a replacement."

"It may take a long time," she looked up and smiled.

"Fine with me," I smiled back.

"Thank you, Lee," she surprised him.

"For what?" he asked.

"For not recording us."

"There's no money in it," I joked.

Kind of.

The immortal eventually finds he is not afraid of what people will do to him if they find out. He's afraid of what of what people will think. He's afraid of being a disappointment. They'll think he's boring. Since he doesn't seem to have the ability to pass on his genes, or whatever keeps him going, he has nothing else to hold their attention but a life of avoiding stories worth telling. He debates making things up, stealing stories from the history he has learned. He rationalizes the possibility. He watches and reads and listens to history, after all, to see if anything stirs. Maybe he should start to make certain that happens. Once his physical immortality is verified, no one can prove his stories are wrong if he goes back far enough, as long as he keeps them simple, light on details, and heavy on feelings. Which is what happens to stories, anyway. They undergo a rewrite with each revisit. Particulars fade and sentiments rise. Events migrate from the mind to the midsection. What happened on a certain date or during a distinct era won't be what they want from him. That's what historians are for. How it felt to be there will be his domain. He needs to be selective. He can't pretend to have been in too many places. He needs to establish a timeline and geography closely aligned with the sequence he is used to, but emphasize particularly traumatic or outlandish events, the kind that would make sense to still remember even centuries later, at least to those who never had to live forever. The immortal feels better about producing new layers by knowing they are based on what is true, and the truth is that nothing much changes by the day. Daily life is the child we raise and don't notice the minor updates happening until years pass. His fairy tales zoom in on the satisfaction of small jobs well done, tasks accomplished, errands run. He places them in proximity to historical set pieces, and claims they didn't know those episodes were happening until days, sometimes weeks later. Like the time he was living in Mexico during the Civil War and some of the young locals rode into Texas to see if they could fight for whichever side let them in. They felt like they were slowly dying in the fields, in the sun, and wanted to either speed it up, or have something to talk about. They saw no beauty in daily goals. None of them came home. When everyone they left behind finally learned that Lincoln had been assassinated weeks after it happened, after his funeral train had made its run and his remains were buried, their family and friends stopped waiting for them. The immortal saw similar scenarios unfold in every place to which he migrated. History broke out in the background while life hummed along in the foreground, with a curious few jumping into the big picture to see what they could see before being swept away. This is not a lie. He merely changes what is in the background and foreground, and who jumps. Nobody expects him to remember their names, so he doesn't have to make up any. All he has to let them know is that there is nobility in the humdrum and that the spectacular is rather discriminating with regard to who ends up as a statue.

•••

Devon designed enough online prattle so that sales climbed and the number of people filling the folding chairs at readings could be referred to as an audience, if not a crowd. Stirred by her ability to manipulate the future, I consumed her tips on how to play my part.

She suggested I grow more enigmatic, an embodiment of the book, in relation to the growth of spectators. I was told to just read, with no banter or exposition between passages, and to say nothing other than "thank you" during signings. If someone asked what the inscription "You Already Know" means, I would smile as if to say they already knew.

Lee needed to go back and tend to his own flock, but finding someone to shoot video was easy enough. Every town I toured had at least one college, so Devon would contact the Chair of a Social Sciences Department and have them send over a student who would claim the evening as an internship.

My resignation from Libby's house was amicable. She said I could come back when all of this shriveled up.

"Like you," I got in one last jab, much to her delight.

For the two months I was on the road, I didn't have to worry about finding a place to stay. When the tour was complete, I took up residence on Devon's compound in one of the many rooms so we could plan the upcoming conferences.

They were touted as chances to deeply explore the themes of the book with like-minded readers, with a warning that space was limited. We denied some requests. The denials had nothing to do with space availability, but rather their responses to the question all applicants had to answer: What do you think is the moral of the story?

Four interpretations emerged from the submissions. Some hopefuls expressed it in a single line, others over the course of many pages, but most of them ultimately fit into one of the brackets which we labeled with working titles that sounded like game show categories:

1) Live Fast

2) Live Slow

3) God?

4) God!

Initially we had a fifth called "Don't Fear The Reaper", but came to realize nearly every entry could be stacked into that pile.

Those not making the cut included some who took the book at face value and said it simply proves immortals walk amongst us, and along those lines, a small faction of amateur Biblical scholars who weren't focused on God so much as a determination to prove the ages assigned to certain people in certain pages of the Old Testament. There was a smattering of space aliens, including assertions that the book demonstrates humans are not native to Earth. Most of the parties we tossed were clearly incorporating *The Logistics of Immortality* within larger manifestos they had been modifying and sharing for years. Many of the rejected also included links to videos they had produced to illuminate their ideas. Whenever Lee came over, the three of us would watch some of them until our heads hurt from laughter and disbelief.

We further delineated the groups based on location. The conferences were our live forays into the major markets. Devon rented hotel ballrooms in a pool of big cities.

A keynote speaker, one of the blurb mouthpieces dusted off from the book jacket, would kick off the weekend. They were chosen based on how close they lived to a given location. Due to a glut of Los Angeles and New York residents, some had to be flown to other locales, but we were able to keep the travel expenses reasonable. The contract allowed speakers to discuss whatever they wanted, so long as they somehow connected their work to the book within the first fifteen minutes of their speech and maintained the relationship throughout. They were also allotted a book signing station on the second day, if they had been published within the past year.

When the spotlight swung away from the keynote address, the attendees would be funneled into surrounding conference rooms for breakout sessions based on their responses to the question regarding the story's meaning. Lee served as moderator for one of the sessions dedicated to the existence of God as often as he could, depending on his church obligations, while the remaining mods were academics from the nearest universities. Devon also jumped in and moderated some sessions. She preferred those concerned with living slowly. The breakouts were designed to function like Socratic classroom discussions, so she enjoyed the feeling of being back in her original environment, and discovering her game still had flair.

I was to enhance my air of mystery. Per instructions, I would enter the keynote delivery late, and stand in the back near the doors to allow for gradual recognition. A slow succession of heads would turn, then lean into the heads beside them and gesture in my direction. I was always sure to exit right before the conclusion of the speech, then silently appear at each breakout session with nothing but a nod exchanged between me and the moderator. I was never introduced. When anyone in attendance asked a moderator if I was me, they would say yes, but offer no information if pressed, other than to emphasize my reclusiveness. I was afraid of coming across as aloof, so I cultivated a pensive resting face for my strolls and a sheepish smile for when inadvertent eye contact was made.

The first round of sessions were agreeable by nature, as we grouped them based on their shared beliefs as to what the book meant. Most of their efforts revolved around compiling evidence in support of their contention, both from the book itself, and any outside source material they had synthesized while contemplating their take. The groups gravitated toward philosophy and non-fiction for backup, as if to ground their spin in reality. For instance, the Live Fast gangs leaned on existentialists along the lines of Camus and de Beauvoir, and often referenced a roster of luminaries who either died young or overstayed their welcome. The Live Slow teams invoked the likes of Locke and Rousseau, the Social Contract, and some contemporary food writers. Those leery of God's existence blended the book's pages with modern atheists such as Hitchens, Harris, and Dawkins, while those who saw God's work in the life of the immortal cited classical theologians like Saint Augustine and Thomas Aquinas. The Don't Fear The Reaper types, who were scattered throughout, shared cultures that are reputed to have a healthy relationship with death, and frequently relied on the Buddhist notion of the self being nonexistent. I couldn't say how convincing any of their cases were. I didn't have the kind of education to mentally check their work, but they all seemed confident, and rare was the moderator, including Devon and Lee, who made any behind-the-back comments about them in passing.

After lunch, which I ate out of sight, since watching someone eat is very demystifying, the groups were broken up. New teams were composed of members from opposing factions. Each freshly-minted subset of the new group put their heads together before presenting their case to the rest. After all divisions had defended their thesis, the group debated which one was most convincing. This led to an even sturdier relationship between members and their ideas. If their mind was changed, they understood the ability to sympathize with an opposing view is characteristic of a strong critical thinker. If their perspective withstood debate, they understood the ability to craft an ironclad argument is characteristic of a strong critical thinker. A win-win for all, maybe a rationalization-rationalization. Either way, they came out of the conversations more devout than they came in, ready to vie for a meeting with me.

Before breaking for the first day, they each responded to a new question: Do you think adults and children respond differently to the concept of immortality? Does one group embrace the thought of being immortal, while the other rejects it? Which does which? Or do you think the responses would be similar for the most part? Why?

Their answers determined who earned invitations for a one-on-one on day two. The runners-up would still participate in workshops focused on applying their ideas to their personal and professional lives, but at no point would Lee or Devon approach them from behind, tap them on the shoulder, and tell them I was waiting in the executive suite.

•••

The immortal cannot be too much of anything. Being too withdrawn or too jovial draws attention. He is a reliable employee, social to a tepid degree. He attends parties when invited, but does not go out for beers after work. He keeps his residence tidy but not immaculate. When renting a house, he keeps the weeds down in front, but plants no flowers. He drives very defensively. He has not been in a major accident since the invention of the automobile. During the occasional parking lot do-si-do, if someone is belligerent with him, he remains calm but firm. Yelling back escalates, slinking away encourages. His walk is deliberate. He never runs. He avoids being that guy who does a certain thing. That jogger, dog walker, bicyclist, complainer, that guy with the metal detector, the guy who always wears that hat. His work clothes are always dirty, so people look the other way. His off-the-clock clothes are neither in style nor out. T-shirts, polo shirts, collared, all solid colors, nothing dramatic, navy and light blue, brown and white, with jeans and khakis. Enough variety to not be associated with wearing the same thing too frequently. No logos. He does not want to give the impression of favoring anything. His vision is fine, he's never needed glasses, but if he did, he would not order any bright-colored frames. They would be black, like his sunglasses. He drives mid-size sedans, buys them used, and pays cash. He pays cash for everything. It leaves no mark, unless it's a large amount, so other than a car every five years, which is about the biggest-ticket item people pay for in cash, he avoids indulgences. Food is the one essential that allows for some expression, at least in private. The ingredients are not particularly eye-catching, a quotidian line of items gliding down the conveyer belt toward the cashier at the grocery store, but his knack for blending them into culinary kaleidoscopes is the strongest indicator of a lengthy life outside of his talent for building landscapes. The specific influences escape him, it's rather a feeling of having walked and ridden and sailed across most of the world. Like so much in his deep well of experience, he can only guess at what exactly lies far below the surface. His dishes don't have names. They are his. His cooking is the one thing he can imagine preventing him from being a total bore should he be revealed, should the stories he concoct not connect. Sometimes he imagines having a show on one of those home and garden networks. And while he wouldn't be able to trace the cultural origins of his creations, he would have guests on who could tell him. He could start to retrace his path in front of an audience, piece together his past on camera, accomplish what he could not through hypnosis and history. Or he may stump even the most well-versed foodie, prove to be the most extreme example of multiculturalism and globalism, all the points on his map coming together to render fruitless any attempts at differentiation. Then he remembers that carrying a show requires charisma. Maybe they could hire a host to narrate his actions. Someone who might be able to make him look exciting.

Nearly every answer from the conference hopefuls had kids far more intrigued with immortality than adults. And as some responses went on to articulate, in so many words, the younger the child, the greater the intrigue. Life already seems long to them. As one respondent analogized, they're waiting in line for adulthood, standing, fidgeting, pining for the ride to start. When they finally get on, they want it to last forever. Assuming a relatively normal childhood, they have yet to meet the grind. They only anticipate the privileges of adulthood, all those exciting places denied them, the ride they've been watching from afar that makes everyone laugh and scream.

The arguments were uniformly convincing, the participants having been through a day of defending themselves, so we based our invites on articulation. Devon and Lee established criteria that considered how often they used their own lives as evidence. The point was to find those who were keenly interested in meeting me in order to talk about themselves. Upon filtering their responses to seek the self-absorbed, our final cuts valued emotion over reason.

"They're all eloquent, all logical," Devon said during our first selection. "But some invest more passion than others. That's what we're looking for."

"People who don't just want to be read," Lee added. "They want to be heard."

"By you," Devon emphasized. "Look for key words that reveal their devotion."

"To my work."

"You," she insisted.

"They don't know me."

"They think they do," Devon said.

"They want to," Lee said.

I think that's who said what. They spoke at the same time.

Up until then, the process had been surprising, often pleasantly so, but the idea that anyone saw me as having anything to offer other than a short book with a morbid sense of humor was baffling, and a more prominent clue than the previous ones that I should have stopped the affair before it started.

Devon and Lee reminded me before each block of meetings to listen and ask questions, to let the students guide themselves. Every time they recited this reminder, I thought of the expression about how it's better to remain silent and be thought of as a fool than speak and remove all doubt. It didn't quite fit, since the people who sat across from me didn't think I was a fool. I wondered how badly I would have to blow it for them to realize it did fit, that I was a fool, what I could say or do to change their minds short of farting and giggling my way through their confessions, which is how the one-on-ones came across. All I needed was a screen between us, a cassock over my business casual wardrobe, and a prescription for Hail Marys. They felt guilty over how they had utilized their talent and work ethic, a gnawing over having spent a significant amount of time on a youthful fantasy, a career not necessarily bad, but a bad fit.

Sessions would last thirty minutes, twenty-nine of them filled with the voice of the latest winner.

"I owned a college admissions consulting firm," one woman told me, which sounded like a noble enough pursuit. "But what I really did was provide tips on how to maintain the status quo of wealth and privilege and squash social mobility."

"Oh."

"For ten thousand dollars," she lamented. "I designed ideal candidates for prestigious schools from families who could afford me. One of the choice qualities is ability to pay tuition, and not force the school to dip into any foundation money, so that part was already taken care of. But we still had to build an appealing application. If they didn't have the academic chops for a four-point-whatever GPA with shiny

SAT and ACT scores, I referred them to some stellar tutoring and test prep services. For the extracurricular bona fides, I recommended sports played in rich enclaves so they'd only be competing with each other, things like water polo, fencing, lacrosse, tennis, golf. If their kid was more the artsy type, something expensive like ballet, oil painting, sculpture, or getting involved with the most well-funded theatre company nearby. Student government helps, of course, but races for office at an elite high school can be competitive, so I often served as something of a campaign adviser, which might involve some pricey promotions and get-out-the-vote incentives. For off-campus activities to show their preferred colleges what great people they are, I emphasized altruism and sensitivity."

"That sounds nice."

"It does. But does volunteering ten hours a week or flying to Honduras for charity sound like the kind of thing a kid can afford to do who has to work to help her family pay the bills? An unpaid internship may signal your interest in a career for something more than money, but not caring about money is easier when you don't have to worry about it. Are you sensing a pattern in all of the above?"

I did, but wasn't sure whether shaking my head or nodding it was the appropriate reaction.

"I was undefeated. A one hundred percent success rate. They didn't always get into the college with the five percent acceptance rate, but they went somewhere good enough, a fifteen to twenty. Good enough to stay in the club. Good enough to maintain their legacy."

Then there was the video game developer who designed a world that existed in the blind spots in our field of vision, where rods and cones make way for the optic nerve and blood vessels that block what those parts of our eye can see, so we fill in the blanks based on the surrounding visuals, our blind spot becoming an assumption based on what is already being seen.

"But what if it isn't?" he asked, as though taking me through his original sales pitch. "What if the blind spot is really a portal into a different dimension? A world right in front of our face, but invisible. The same environment, but in heightened colors and contrasts, which we were able to portray, by the way, rather brilliantly. The filters and palettes we used made it look next-level. But what happened in this dimension, that was even cooler. It's where all the events you quickly imagine happening as you look at something or someone, but quickly dismiss, actually happen. Where you really do ram the pickup with the truck nuts that just cut you off in traffic, the hot server really does approach your table naked to take your order, you do walk off the job while tossing the perfect one-liner at your boss, but the visible world is still your default setting. The alternate reality accessible through your blind spot leaves no consequences. You visit it in short bursts. Of course, it's not actually you doing all this. It's the characters in the game. Still, fun concept. Right?"

I nodded.

"As far as the plot and objective were concerned, I wanted to run with the cerebral nature of the premise, wrap it in a story of someone who uses it to perfect their career path, or a relationship, or even the perfect crime. Simulate the different directions they can take and apply the sims to a best case scenario. Players would choose a character and a narrative from a variety of options. The more options, the higher the budget. That bothered my investors. They wanted me to limit the number. They claimed nobody would choose the more life-like threads, so why not just roll the with the crime and the action? I understood. But I wanted to make something unique. A game that could adopt someone's personality. We create these worlds only to serve a plot that has to do with someone trying to destroy it, or use it for diabolical purposes. We barely explore its capabilities before we have to defend it. Why can't we let it be? Do what it's meant to do?"

I shrugged.

"I caved. Too much money on the table. Too many people relying on me to get paid. I worked my ass off day and night for something I didn't believe in. The world inside our blind spot looked fantastic. But it was just a setting, a backdrop, a cool backstory leading up to the same old shit. Shoot them before they shoot you. You much of a gamer?"

I shook my head.

"I was going to ask if you've heard of it, but pretty much only serious gamers have. I sold out, but didn't cash in. It has a cult following. Once it became clear we weren't going to live up to the earnings forecast, I gave as many interviews as I could, posted a history of its development, told anyone who would listen about what it was supposed to be. I think that helped. Gave it some lore, a legend that made people who knew about it feel smart. The thing itself may not be interesting, but the image of it is."

He said that's why he admired the book. He could tell the promotion was true, that it was written without any regard for commercial appeal, before I met Devon and her legion. It came across as somewhat of a backhanded compliment, which was more than I could say for his thoughts on Devon, which were neither ambiguous nor complimentary.

She had warned me about a strain of resentment that would sometimes surge through the cracks of a conference. Even those most grateful for help wish they didn't need it. So many of them worked in the kinds of careers we are raised to pursue. Lawyers of all kind were well-represented.

A former District Attorney was trying to like people again. She ran for Attorney General of her state, won the primary, but lost the general election, along with any sense of pride in being a human being.

"We're the worst," she said. "Name a species worse than us."

I felt like saying squid. I shrugged so often during the sessions that my arms felt like tentacles. But I refrained. I shrugged. She wasn't really asking me, anyway. And I didn't know enough about squid to disparage them like that.

"Every living thing pretty much just eats and fucks. But the non-humans contribute something. A food source, an equalizer, but what do we have to offer? Anecdotes. Stories of rescue dogs and whales freed from fishing nets. They wouldn't be in those predicaments in the first place if it wasn't for us. What do we contribute to anyone or anything other than ourselves?"

She was the type who liked to talk in questions.

"I should have known. I did know. I was a public defender for seven years, a DA for five more. My district was pretty nondescript. People complained. They always complained. Everything was my fault. But it was about things, about laws, crimes, construction projects, schools. Occasional bouts of personal insults, but nothing, and I mean nothing, like when I made the mistake of running for higher office. I understood the concept of evil thanks to some cases I worked on, but I was always hearing things second-hand. The kind of behavior I had encountered in person up until that point was simply lazy or disappointing, but frustrating enough to confuse it with something worse. Once the campaign started, I became well-acquainted with genuine cruelty and depravity on a personal level. It wasn't about things anymore. It was about me. The comment threads on my social media were horrifying enough, but the emails? My God. My aides offered to run interference for me, screen the most terrible and keep them away, but I wanted to see it all. I needed to know whom I was expected to serve. I'd give them credit for creativity if I suspected any of their rape and murder fantasies were made up. But they were way too specific, way beyond the pay grade of someone willing to devote that much time to a comment thread or inbox. These were actual dreams they had. I'm certain of this. They were mostly men, of course, but I was just as pissed at the women who raised them, who didn't set them straight when they had the chance, and at the women who dated or married them because they thought it was better than being alone. By the time election day rolled around, I didn't want to fight for people. I wanted to get rid of them. I was relieved when I lost. I was afraid of what I might do with any measure of power. I couldn't file any lawsuits. Where would I start? Which one of the hundreds, maybe thousands, would I start with? And if I did choose one, make an example of him, how would the others respond? What kind of rallying cry would I become? With all those pitfalls in mind, then, what other courses of action would I have? Which ones would I seriously consider?"

That was one of the moments when I didn't have to prevent myself from responding. I was at a sincere loss, and wondered how anything we had to offer could possibly help her, much less anything I could say.

Different types of lawyers were exposed to different stressors leading to the same ends. One had grown tired of finding ways for his client to hide the obscene amount of money he had inherited, which may not have been so bad if the client didn't carry himself as some kind of business wizard whose ingenuity had made him rich, rather than a genetic crap shot. Another specialized in helping the large corporation she worked for navigate through myriad regulations, while at the same time lobbying to make sure even more regulations were passed so that smaller competitors who couldn't afford people like her would give up.

I was expecting more people from finance, but was told by one of them that as time passed, more money consolidated into fewer hands. This tightening of their circle made it easier to size each other up, which according to my source, led to more crises than the possibility of their jobs becoming obsolete.

A psychiatrist seized on the financier's lament as the theme of her sit-down. I sat and silently related as she considered closing her practice because she had grown tired of listening to successful people complain about their lives.

"They compare themselves to their peers all the time," she said. "The competitive drive that helps them get what they want prevents them from enjoying it once they get there. Do you remember the biggest, toughest guy at your high school?"

I could not, but nodded anyway.

"The one who really liked to fight?"

I continued to pretend.

"He eventually picked a fight with the wrong person, didn't he?"

I didn't bother nodding anymore since she didn't seem to notice my previous efforts.

"He found someone bigger and tougher than him. He didn't want to. He never imagined losing, but it was bound to happen since he liked to fight so much. So he learned there were bigger bad asses out there thanks to that one beatdown. Meanwhile, my patients do this to themselves constantly. Several beatdowns a day. They pick fights with people who don't even know they're being fought. It's passive and internal and unnecessary. Successful people shouldn't judge themselves against other successful people. They should judge themselves against unfortunate people, then thank God, then shut up. That's what they should do, but should is a nonsense word. Should is gibberish."

She was right. And Devon was right. The right thing is almost always obvious. I felt as though instead of writing "You Already Know" when signing copies of the book, I should write "No Shit". Rarely were any of the people who spoke to me dealing with problems out of their control. Self-help and self-harm were of a piece, a flirtatious couple playfully arguing on the phone over who should hang up first.

When another doctor sat across from me later and expressed satisfaction and appreciation for his career, I nearly fell back in my chair. He was a surgeon, and he feared for the future of his profession. The hospitals in which he performed were gravitating toward robotics for some of the more routine surgeries, and he gathered more complexity was coming. He never thought his skills would be subject to automation. "Like some assembly line worker, or call center grunt," as he put it, making him less sympathetic and easier to listen to impassively.

I didn't hear much when he ruminated on his next move, where he would go should he decide to make a change, as it was with the other doctors and lawyers and managers and owners when they mulled over their futures. It was more talk, something they were good at, nothing they acted upon, not in their professional lives. They had pulled plenty of plugs in their personal lives, ended many a relationship. But their careers sauntered on.

They never told me they were interested in working for us. I guess they assumed that was Devon's department. I was the sage, she was the sage manager. When she said she was considering turning her ranch into a center or an institute of some sort, thanks to all the offers she was receiving from the professionals who attended our conferences and wanted to help make it happen, my first impulse was to joke with Lee as to what we should call it.

"The Center for Immortality?"

"The Should Center?"

"The No Shit Center?"

But when it became clear nobody else was joking, I wondered how often I would be allowed out of my room, or whether I would even want to leave it.

The immortal attends immortality conventions. He likes to hear about the latest research and mingle with people who want to live forever. The word 'immortality' isn't used very often. Acolytes of the movement want to be taken seriously, and the word may suggest sci-fi or fantasy. Maybe the companies and organizations involved are wary of overpromising and underperforming, so they invent euphemisms. Instead of immortality, they say 'reverse aging', 'radical life extension', or 'unlimited future'. The new vocabulary strikes the immortal as fitting, since none of their visions resembles his life. Their unlimited futures involve nanotechnology, gene editing, and tech interface. Microscopic robots floating through the body to wipe out intruders, repair damage, and suppress white blood cell insurgencies. Splicing and dicing double helixes to fashion designer DNA that keeps the cells dividing. Uploading consciousness into computers and becoming one with artificial intelligence. Many of the presentations define immortality as living much longer than current expectations, but not indefinitely. One of the ethicists featured at one of the larger cons noted that we have a 1-in-1000 chance per year of dying by accident, so we are unlikely to make it to a thousand years, and should therefore set our expectations at two to three hundred. Hearing this makes the immortal question how long he's really lived. He only has hard evidence for about as many years as the guest speaker preached as the maximum. Maybe his time is almost up. His luck is due to run out soon. Or he's finally about to get lucky. His perception of luck depends on his mood. Then a researcher at another convention discusses how lobsters appear to hardly age at all by the time they die naturally, as though they are young their whole lives, which can last over fifty years, then suddenly drop dead. A theory for why the lobster resists aging, the theory that resonates most with the immortal, is based on its slow lifestyle. Unlike humans, which have to keep moving and spend a lot of energy in order to survive, lobsters lead a sedentary, mellow life, which allows them to spend their evolutionary capital on fighting the aging process. The immortal cackles when he first hears this, loudly enough so that he has to whisper some quick apologies to the nearby dirty lookers. Lying low is the immortal's credo. But according to the lobster, avoiding detection to hide his curse also prolongs it. When he talks to people while wandering the convention floor between seminars, many of them are defiant. "Aging is an appeal to tradition," is a common refrain. "It's all we've known as a species, so we've adapted to think that's just the way it is." Another one claims, "Eternal life is pointless without eternal youth." The immortal agrees with the point about youth, as in not-elderly, thanks to his relative good health. Living so long has been hard enough in decent shape. He sees no point in prolonging infirmity. Let the lobster be our guide. The conventioneers assume perpetual vitality, if not youth, when discussing the ethics of the future for which they yearn. Those are the immortal's favorite conversations to eavesdrop on and engage. Much of his enjoyment has to do with participating in a world where he is not alone, if only in the abstract, and if only for a matter of minutes. But the talks are also quite interesting on their own, apart from his all-too-relevant perspective. The questions that most compel the immortal concern wealth and resources. Will radical life extension only be for the rich? Is limiting access actually preferable, given the potential effect that extended life cycles will have on resources? Will more people living much longer force us into population management? Or will innovation save the planet? He dismisses ideas related to interfacing with technology, and uploading our consciousness. He may not enjoy being eternal, but at least he's experiencing it. Watching eternity through a camera or screen, or some kind of hardware, sounds terrifyingly dull. Tactile senses are the most bearable feature of his life sentence. Food, sex, swims, saunas, breezes of all temperatures, even the emotions associated with speculating on his condition. For all his observing, he has still lived.

So he avoids the artificial intelligence roundtables and zeroes in on the ethical dilemmas that have a body. He waits to see which point of view becomes the majority in a given debate, then adopts the opposing side in order to stay stimulated. He knows every angle intimately. It's a subject he has thought of and studied for hundreds of years, perhaps thousands, but not only is his memory limited, so is the research. Both fall back only so far before running into conjecture and delusion. And while he argues from every direction, he is most passionate when responding to the potential drawbacks of reverse aging. His defense of further research has been honed and sharpened and feels the most convincing to him. He can cheer on the committed in their dream of making immortality mainstream by soothing anxieties over social orders based on life expectancy and resources stretched beyond their limits. He was surprised by this passion for unlimited futures when it first started to overtake him, considering his fraught relationship with his own radically extended life. Now he understands. He wants to be like everyone else someday. It may not happen in their lifetimes, but could very well happen in his.

Devon had the final say on the name. Her company would be responsible for the center, after all, and it was centered on her property. She decided to call it the Institute for Personal Action, or IPA. She appreciated that the initials were the same as a craft beer, since she wanted to create an atmosphere that celebrated life while in the process of changing it.

"Like home," she said. "But a home where things get done."

Food and libations were not simply for fun. They were there to lubricate the gears that needed to turn in order for a guest to fulfill their plan of action. She insisted we never say 'plan'. It was always a 'plan of action'. One of our mottos was that you can't have one without the other.

Not that we had many mottos. Our parties arrived with their plans already in place. They were required to submit a plan as part of their application, in addition to a proposal for what service they wanted to provide the IPA while in residence, as we were not charging a fee to attend. The idea was to barter their expertise for ours.

We intended to review the applications thoroughly, with all three of us independently looking over each one, assigning it a score, cutting those with the lowest combined tallies, then revisiting the remainders before meeting to rank them. But the applicant pool was far bigger than we anticipated, so we instead based our selections exclusively on what they intended to do for us. What they planned on doing for themselves became an afterthought.

An architect offered to design an addition to Devon's house that would serve as a conference center. A television producer associated with a show on the tiny house movement offered to scoop up some tiny houses in foreclosure to scatter about Devon's property as guest residences. The game developer who had offered me his backstory of woe offered to build the institution a network to track the progress of residents as they worked toward completion of their plans and provide a communications platform for the IPA. They were all accepted for admission with barely any back-and-forth, other than to gush over how awesome the conference center, guest houses, and network were going to be. Many applicants wanted to donate time and labor related to their field, such as the doctors, therapists, and lawyers who offered to insure the institute was qualified and legitimate. Others expressed a desire to work far away from their field, hoping that tending the grounds, looking after the longhorns, or helping build the construction projects would take their minds off their careers long enough to fulfill their plans, which often involved a new direction in life. They wanted to empty their heads in order to refill them.

We first communicated with the producers, developers, and architects to lay the groundwork for what would eventually be assembled by those who simply wanted to work. Devon and Lee used their local pull to push through the permit process.

As our roster arrived, I wasn't required to be as enigmatic for this round. In creating the jolly ambiance, we were to let our guard down, signaling to the chosen they were allowed behind the curtain, meeting us in the middle as fellow professionals. Devon established only one rule.

"Don't fuck anybody."

She made the announcement one evening as she and I hiked her land to fill the water troughs.

"You mean literally?" I asked.

"It's a slang term. It's never literal."

"Which definition are you referring to?"

"The original. Sexual intercourse."

"Me?" I laughed under the crackle of our footsteps snapping the brittle grass and fallen oak leaves. "You know my history. Or lack of history."

"You've never been in a position like you're about to be in."

"You weren't concerned at the conferences."

"Those were highly monitored, regimented environments. This is a retreat. Designed for a certain kind of intimacy. Please keep it to that certain kind."

"Okay."

"I mean it."

"Okay."

We took our voices out of our walk and gave way to the sounds around us until the next stop was in sight.

"Why so adamant?" I asked.

"About sex? Why do you think?"

"You're jealous."

She didn't break her stride. I tried again.

"It's a bad look."

"How so?"

"It's sleazy."

My answer was too easy. She was not satisfied with it.

"We're entering tricky territory here, Luca."

We came upon the watering station. She unraveled the hose and dropped it into the half-full trough before turning it on.

"I've never taken things this far," she stared into the swirling surface. "I'm confident we're doing it right, but we need to always be aware of perceptions. We want to avoid the c-word."

"I swear," I reiterated. "No sex with the guests."

"Not that c-word," she rolled her eyes. "Do you really think I'd ever use that term for anything associated with women?"

"Of course not," I smirked.

She caught on, shook her head, and included a smirk of her own.

I reverted back to sincerity.

"You mean 'cult', yes?"

She turned off the spigot.

"Yes."

We headed back in the direction of the house.

"It's why we're keeping money out of it. The free labor and donations won't be a problem so long as guests are free to leave whenever they want. Nobody can accuse us of fraud or isolation. The philosophy is driven by the participants. We're not presenting an alternate reality, not demanding they believe us and only us. All we have left to do is avoid any hint of trading in sex, which may be the hardest part."

"Come on, Devon."

"I know, I know," she was starting to breathe harder thanks to talking while hiking. "You have no moves, no game, you've damn near been a monk most of your life. But you won't need any moves. The opportunities will present themselves. Your history may indicate discipline, but that history could also be lost time you decide to make up for."

"I would think you'd have an opinion on that by now."

"Of course I do. We're moving ahead, aren't we?"

"Thank you," I took an extra breath as we scaled a small hill. "I won't let you down."

"I'm just doing some last-minute fretting. Making sure everything is in place."

"I understand."

I did.

Woodpeckers chattered and chased each other above us, darting between oak trees in a fight over the holes pitted in the trunks and branches.

I understood her alarm, but was certain I could squint into the shimmer of short-term temptation.

Then our invention came to life and challenged that conviction.

The retreat was like a lengthy vacation at a summer rental, a languid resurrection where people could try on a new identity amongst others who weren't aware of the one they normally wore. Our guests were all smart and often physically attractive, because so much of their success was based on people wanting to be near them.

The work we did was invigorating, and I don't mean the work of our guests planning their life changes. The most satisfying tasks involved transforming the ranch from a beautiful piece of land into paradise.

We would spend maybe an hour in the morning conducting the business of the brochure. After breakfast, our guests would find a place to work privately or in small groups: a corner of the great room in the main house, a cluster of patio furniture in the yard, a tiny house. Devon and Lee and I would fan out and circulate amongst them, asking how things were going, then nodding and furrowing our brows as they responded. They would fiddle with their plans, project how the plan would apply to a variety of scenarios in their life, and since they were perfectionists, fiddle with them some more since a change in one led to changes in the other.

When the fiddling became counterproductive, they saved their work and the best part of the day would begin. We would help build the conference wing on the main house, help hook up the water and power to the tiny houses, help tend to the land, help fix lunch and deliver it to the various worksites, help prepare and organize dinner. Our duties would rotate. We huddled and discussed what needed to be done that day, then decided who would work where. The only complaints came from those who wanted to perform more than one task, which were quickly mitigated as people agreed to swap jobs after lunch.

I sometimes wonder if that time and place even existed, or if it was a virtual reality program designed by engineers who spend their evenings playing in bands and performing open mic comedy who wanted to provide their peers with an authentic yet comfortable experience: hygienic hippie, electric Amish. I helped raise one of the walls of the conference center one afternoon. When we finished walking it up into place, the man who had gripped the beam next to me said "I've never felt more productive" as we stood back, gulped air, and watched our colleagues nail the frame to the others. I patted him on the back and tried to remember his real-world occupation, with the idea of cracking a joke about how much more satisfying this was than analyzing input or generating output, but could not recall what he did. We were blending, becoming a force.

Dinners were spectacular. The food was fresh, prepared with whatever the meal team found most appealing when they went into town for ingredients. It was always served family-style, large platters of pasta and vegetables and grilled fish and game ranging across the middle of the table flanked by bottles of red wine and hunks of bread. White wine, water, and beer bobbed in tubs of ice that surrounded the patio. Coming off a day of demanding labor made it all the more nourishing. Blue collar days followed by white collar nights.

The conversations were just as nourishing, substance peppered with quick wit. The subjects seldom concerned current events, unless what was happening in the news could be used to illustrate a point about the great film being discussed, or philosophical tradition, or scientific concept. I had a hard time keeping up, but didn't mind, as I wasn't expected to contribute much. They seemed to want my approval rather than to hear from me. My role still largely involved wandering about slowly while offering wise nods of acknowledgement, like an ambulatory Buddha statue.

Not everyone jumped on board. Some who wanted more traditional retreat time, rather than actually retreating, left soon after they realized the IPA wasn't what they expected. Others were appreciative enough, but didn't see the need to stick around once they had their plan in place. They were a fraction of the whole number of guests. Their departures would not have made a discernable difference in a group photo, plus we gained almost as many as we lost based on referrals from those who stayed, and believed in what we were doing, whatever it was we were doing.

The circumstances made it easy to fall for someone, for however long. Guests frequently paired up and disappeared into an upstairs room, tiny house, or oak grove. Plans were drafted to create a small lake on the ranch, or maybe it was a large pond, ostensibly for an emergency water reserve and to stock with fish, but when I joked it was really for late night swims, people didn't laugh all that loudly.

I was no exception, hardly the prophet mascot people imagined, except for my insistence on not following through whenever I fell infatuated. With each refusal, honoring Devon's edict became easier, and even started to feel invigorating. I was proud to avoid the awkward aftermaths so many of the others put themselves through. The hookups were probably the biggest drawback for many of our residents. A few may have even left thanks to hurt feelings or embarrassment, but most of the others didn't have to grit their teeth long before they were stealing away with someone else, or at peace with their choices and the partners involved in those decisions. I watched these passion plays carry on, pleased with my discipline. One woman even thanked me for my resolve, for preventing her from compromising her experience. I humblebragged to Lee and expressed my gratitude to Devon for the opportunity to finally and fully fathom the benefits of long-term serenity over immediate gratification.

Then I met Mildred.

We exchanged our first glance during a morning session I was lurking around, since it was in the great room just downstairs from my bedroom. She was one of four members each assessing the current state of their plan, ostensibly looking for feedback from the others, but more likely looking for validation. The architect of the conference center was a quarter of the foursome. As part of an apology he offered over possibly hogging too much of their time, he made pig noises that imitated the sound really well, but lasted long enough to prompt the look between Mildred and me.

"About four seconds too long," was her assessment later that morning after the others went outside.

"I was going to say three," I said. "Four is funnier."

"It's more specific," she proffered. "Three is associated with 'a few', which people say all the time. Like how 'a couple' is two. Four exists more as its own number."

"There's a quartet."

"How often do people use that word?"

"Not very.

"Unless they're classical music fans."

"There's a foursome."

"The number is right there in the word," she took it as further proof.

"Five would also be too standard."

"It's also too high. His snorting did not last five seconds too long. That would be an eternity. Reality is funnier than exaggeration. Most of the time."

I noticed some activity in the kitchen as some guests prepared the lunch boxes.

"What would be a funny price for a burrito?" I asked.

"What kind of burrito? And for what purpose? We need context."

"The inspiration for some expression like 'that's worse than a ninety-nine cent burrito.'"

"It can't be ninety-nine cents," she said in all sincerity.

"No?"

"Too cheap," she started to formulate her analysis. "Too obvious."

"A more specific, offbeat number then."

"Prices fit certain patterns," she shook her head. "Nobody charges x dollars and eighty-seven cents, not before tax. It's ninety-five, or ninety-nine, or whole dollars."

"So what's the answer?"

"I think we need to go general for this one. Maybe three dollars. A boring burrito, which is about the worst thing you can say about one. They're never really bad. Lots of filler at that price. Nothing but beans and rice. Remember we need to ground the number in reality."

"Plus an expression needs the kind of flow and rhythm that a one-syllable number provides," I joined her brainstorm.

"Maybe the expression would be 'more *boring* than a three-dollar burrito.'"

"And three is funnier than four in this case."

"Definitely."

"Because it's a magic number," I unearthed her reason.

"Until you put a dollar sign next to it," she confirmed.

Which was the first round of a game we often played that we may have called Which Number is Funnier if we had named it, and which never actually made us laugh. It was all very analytical. Laughter was a projection, the solution to an equation.

She was not part of the original cohort, arriving as a replacement for a rather efficient older man who felt he had no time to spare on a communal experience at the expense of carrying out the plan he had developed. I loved her name before I had a chance to love anything else about her. "Mildred" sounded old, like she should be older than the man whose space she was filling. I knew this was not the case, having read her application, but when we started to spend time together, her name came to represent a delightful junction of wisdom and age. She must have been one of those children people describe as having an old soul, who someday will be regarded as young at heart when she is elderly. Meanwhile I could not imagine her growing any older than she was when I knew her. She was so invested in every moment she lived. Her short hair still seemed like a statement, as it may have been during a bygone era, rather than one of many styles she had to choose from nowadays. She hopped right into the tide of the retreat and made its ideal all the more idyllic. Groups were enhanced when she was a part of them, activities were energized, and I was grateful for any moment alone with her.

Her professional life was also a brew of old and new: Human Resources Director by day, YouTube personality by night. I didn't ask about her broadcasting persona until we were dozens of conversations deep, covering every acre of the ranch.

"I always talked to myself while I took off my makeup," she explained. "I started to turn a camera on me to see what would happen, if it would be worth posting."

"And was it?"

I asked because I knew her answer would not be defined by her number of followers.

She took her time, looking in the direction of the surveyors who were tracing a likely spot for the pond. Two of them stood behind their tripod at the base of a hill across from us, as though we were squaring off, ready to sprint across the meadow at each other, and they were peering through their scope searching for an advantage.

"It depends on what you mean by worth," she said, then apologized for saying it. "I know that sounds like such a copout, but honestly, I don't know what to think about the whole thing anymore. It's why I'm here."

"What part was the most worthy?"

"The admiration," she answered immediately this time. "It was a very gratifying form of admiration. People, mostly young girls, thanked me for being there for them, for saying things that made them feel better."

She started our walk again, as if anticipating my next question about what wasn't worthy, and wanting to avoid it.

"What were you saying to them?" I asked instead.

She stopped.

"You haven't watched any of my videos?"

"It didn't feel right. It's odd enough I was able to read your application. Outside of the big-time terrible things to be accused of, stalking is something I work hard to avoid."

"And it's so easy to be a stalker nowadays."

"From the comfort of your own home."

"No more crouching in bushes and sitting in trees outside bedroom windows."

"We are in a golden age."

She picked up our stride where she left off.

"Or dark age," I continued. "If you're looking at it from the other direction."

I trailed her and waited for the follow-up, the story of the over-exuberant fan.

"I'm just walking," she said, noting the lilt of anticipation in my voice. "Nobody got dark on me. They were kids. I got dark on myself."

"Any tips you could give me?"

We reached the hill, the one where the surveyors stood at its base a hundred yards to our left, and started to scale it.

"I'm here to get tips, not give them," she said.

"You didn't read our mission statement."

We both used a laugh to start our heavier breathing that the hill required.

"I kept thinking about that theory," she said. "How something doesn't behave the same when you pay attention to it. You're studying a performance."

"So you put on a certain face for the camera. That sounds pretty standard."

"But my whole shtick was keeping it real. That's what all the comments said. *'Love the real talk.'* *'Keep it one hundred.'* *'For real, M. For real.'* And the whole taking off my makeup thing, that forced metaphor. I felt like a liar within a month, but didn't stop. Sometimes I'd shoot several in one day, over the weekend. Re-apply my makeup each time just to take it off, to ramble on about reality, so I'd have enough stored up to feed them during the week since I couldn't bear to do it every night when I got home."

She ran out of breath.

We had made it to the top. We turned to see what the surveyors were looking at below. They continued their discussion, pieces of their voices occasionally piercing the sound of the birds and our breathing. They peered through their instrument every so often, paying us no mind. Short, skinny wooden stakes with pink streamers tied to their tops dotted the gorge yards apart in what seemed like random spots unless you imagined lines between them and started to see a circle.

"So it was the production schedule that got you," I said.

"That, and I was approached about monetizing the channel. I was feeling fake enough, then here comes a mental health non-profit looking to advertise, some teen spirit organization, and a cosmetics company. A cosmetics company. Can you believe that? I asked them, 'Have you watched the channel?' They said it was for their makeup removal products, but I think they were backtracking. Someone in the office finally tuned in while we were on the phone and whispered in their ear."

"It wasn't the pressure of meaning so much to people who didn't know you."

"There weren't that many of them," she inhaled and responded on the exhale. "Yet. Probably enough to fill a large public high school. I wasn't going on tour anytime soon, but I was on my way. And I wasn't responsible for them. I was like a grandma or an aunt who gets to spoil them and make them feel good, then leave."

I saw her point, because she made me feel good, too. I was familiar with her work without having seen it. I was more open to the possibility of embracing my role than I had been since the first evening Devon and Lee took me out for haute cuisine and local wine. Their persuasiveness had worn off the next morning once I was rehydrated and faced with average food. Mildred had me believing, or admitting, that playing guru was a future memory worth creating, and the only enticement she needed to convince me, aside from herself, was fresh air. I imagined the hole that would someday hollow the space beneath us, which would catch rain water trickling down the hill. Maybe it wasn't admiration I feared.

"What does it feel like when your time has passed?" I asked.

"That's what the people close to you are for. They remind you the run never really mattered."

Like so many times before, almost all the time I spent with her, I wanted to kiss her. But if I was to cultivate my inner guru, to follow her implied advice and wear the role I couldn't help poring over and sizing up for imperfections, I had to abide by Devon's request that I remain a platonic figure. Or as she so artfully put it, not fuck anyone.

"On the other hand," I confided in Lee over lunch after his next Sunday service, "I don't have anyone close to me. And I feel like Mildred could be my chance."

We sat in a throwback diner that predated the wine tourism, a place where longtime locals liked to linger and grouse about change.

Lee stared into the distance, into his lack of a response.

"Can you at least let me in on the theme of what you're contemplating?" I asked. "Maybe I can help."

"You need me to be pastorly," he waved me off. "Let me choose my words carefully."

"So you can tell me as diplomatically as possible to lay off her."

"I'm not going there yet. I was thinking of who might be close to you already."

"To no avail."

"If we can think of someone, it might make you feel better, less conflicted."

"If only..."

I swirled a fry in the puddle of ketchup on my plate.

"Your patients," he decided. "The old folks you take care of."

"They might not be around by the time my run is over. Besides, they're the ones who need comfort. They're facing the end of the biggest run of all."

"Which provides some perspective, yes?"

He took a triumphant sip of iced tea.

"We were talking about comfort, not perspective."

"Nobody in foster care?" he asked, though he didn't seem to want to.

I couldn't articulate an answer. The only response I had was a noise that rattled between a scoff and a retch.

He tried again.

"I was going to suggest me and Devon, but thought you'd make the kind of sound you just made."

I made it again.

"Then I thought maybe not Devon, but maybe me."

I considered the nature of our relationship.

My consideration lasted too long.

"If you have to think about it, then I guess not," Lee concluded.

"Sorry," I scrunched up half my face. "Maybe if we kept our friendship online. We were doomed the moment we went into business together."

"If we remained at a distance, you wouldn't be worried about what happens when this ends, and wouldn't have realized you lack close relationships."

I processed what he said and admired it.

"On that note," he leaned into the pause. "Why are you assuming this is going to end?"

"We can only fool people for so long."

"We're not fooling anyone. That's the beauty of what we've built. They seek for themselves, arrive at their own answers. That's why we agreed there's no need to write a sequel. The book is doctrine. It's effectively vague. Saying anything more would ruin it. All you have to do is be there. And that's what people say is the most important thing to do for those who are closest to us. Just be there."

He took another sip of tea, and as I raised my glass to do likewise, I raised it a little higher as though proposing a toast.

"You're not such a bad pastor," I declared.

"This movement, retreat, whatever we're calling it..."

"The IPA," I reminded him.

He pushed past my dig.

"It's really given me a second wind."

"So I should go for Mildred."

"Oh..." he sounded disappointed.

"I shouldn't?"

"I thought we had strayed far enough off topic that you'd forget about it."

"Not a chance," I loved the feeling.

Pastor Lee let loose a long, slow exhale.

"I never wanted to be the third party in a dispute between you and Devon."

"I have no one else to talk to."

"There's that therapist staying in the powder blue tiny house near the lake site."

"I thought she was a talent agent."

"That's her roommate."

"There are two of them in that house?"

"They get along really well."

"I can't talk to her," I said. "She's a client, a guest. I have an image to maintain."

Lee appeared to brace himself.

"Fine," he let go.

"Thank you, Reverend."

He ran his hands over the table as if to turn it into the desk in his office.

"I take it Mildred knows how you feel."

"I'd be surprised if she doesn't."

Lee looked at me as though I had misspelled God.

"There's room for surprise?"

"Oh yes," it struck me as something good.

"Makes sense," his astonishment slackened. "You've known her for what, two weeks?"

"Three."

"Well in that case..."

"A little more than that. Almost a month."

He leaned back as if he had proven something.

"Come on, Lee. It's about more than time. You know that. You've felt it. Chemical reactions are real. Time is an invention."

"You're really starting to sound like a sage. Or like you're smoking some."

I would have slapped my forehead but it wasn't worth the effort.

"A weed joke?" I underlined my look. "That's so tired."

"I meant it as a compliment. The first part. The weed joke just floated in there. Sorry."

"You did what you could with it."

"Thank you. But seriously, you're growing into your role. And I don't mean 'role' as in a part you're playing. You're truly sounding wise."

"Apart from the whirlwind romance."

Lee shifted and sipped from his glass, which was down to more ice than liquid.

"Your intentions are clearly pure," he said. "Devon shouldn't worry about our efforts turning into something unseemly."

"Thank you for noticing."

"Did you notice that you two kind of look alike?"

"Mildred and I?"

"No, you and Devon," he cracked. "Of course you and Mildred."

"Please," I waved him off without a wave. "Don't try to get in my head, creep me out. You said yourself, my intentions are pure."

"But so soon?" he skipped past his mind game. "Not in terms of how long you've known each other, but so early in the process of what we're building."

"Me being in a committed relationship shouldn't have any effect on that."

"You mentioned your image earlier."

"As something of a joke."

"People who commit to us don't see it that way. They appreciate your serene presence. You embody the immortal, the consistency he represents."

"They're too self-absorbed to notice anything other than their own problems."

"That's spiteful," he admonished me. "Sorry if I'm not saying what you want to hear."

"I can't believe you're willing to risk my happiness for your idea of what helps the business model."

"So it's everyone else who's selfish."

"Don't turn the tables, Lee. Please. That's more cliché than a weed joke."

He shifted in his seat, recalibrating his position.

"I know what you're thinking," he said. "Being with Mildred will make you even more serene, more consistent. More immortal, if you will. But I've counseled hundreds of couples over the years. Relationships that start like yours tend to have the opposite effect."

"That start like ours?"

"All fireworks, all the time. Never a dull moment. Fear of a dull moment. They'll aim the fireworks at each other to avoid one."

"I can handle down time. That's all my life has been."

"And did meeting Mildred change that? Or meeting us?"

I felt as though he had stopped talking and instead was performing a card trick I couldn't quite crack.

"I'm not saying it can't work," he continued to deal. "It just doesn't trend in that direction. And nothing will drop you from prophet to some guy who wrote a book faster than a volatile, failed relationship."

He gestured for the check.

"Go for it, Luca," he said as he pulled out his wallet. "But know the risk."

•••

The immortal wishes he could draw or paint. Art would have been a good way to record his experiences, to provide more detail than his paltry journal entries. Nobody would be suspicious of images from a distant past. Even if he scrawled a date on them, he could claim it was part of the aesthetic. Nobody would wonder if those moments happened. Except for the immortal. His drawings would still be interpretations, not photographs. Some real, some conjured. He wouldn't know which were which, be able to tell the dreams from the authentic. Imagination and non-fiction would blend eventually, as they always had. But he would enjoy looking at them.

A pastorly vapor trail cut through my interactions with Mildred after enabling the Pastor in Lee. I wondered how much I could ruin by asking her if she had any thoughts on my affection. Calling the whole thing off before it was a thing grew more tempting. It was the safest option, preserving any eminence I had earned through the book and the ensuing pretense of my presence. Not to mention maintaining my dignity should Mildred dismiss my declaration, possibly with a laugh. I loved her laugh, but the thought of hearing it in that circumstance made me shiver.

I cursed myself at finding the safe way once more appealing. My decisions had always skewed safe. Even the choice to publish and appear as an author was facilitated by others. I did nothing other than post the product online. So much of my life was spent with people who weren't going to be part of it for very long, from foster families to ancient patients. The conferences and retreat provided the most time I had ever spent with people scheduled to be on earth for the same period as me. I talked myself into making more of that opportunity.

"Would I be wrecking anything if I confessed some feelings for you?"

"How could you?" she gestured across the landscape around us.

We had reached the highest peak on Devon's ranch, where we not only saw her oaks and cows sprinkled over the loaves of hills, but some vineyards, olive groves, and almond orchards beyond. The songs of a hundred birds surrounded us and mocked our conversation, but our talk mattered to us.

"As in you couldn't possibly wreck something so beautiful?" I asked. "Or how could you possibly be so stupid as to wreck something so beautiful?"

She scanned the environment and laughed without a sound.

"I have a confession, too," she said.

"If we keep trading confessions, we never have to deal with what we're confessing," I kept her beauty in the foreground and the scenery in the background. "I like it."

"I was at one of your readings."

"A lot of people here came to a reading."

"But they probably didn't act as weird as I did," she proceeded.

"Nonsense."

"No," she insisted. "I was nuts."

"I would have remembered."

"I was in line to have you sign my copy, and that's when it started. I dropped out of the line, then got back in. I wanted to say something witty when I met you, but couldn't think of anything. I was freaking out. A friend of mine was there, and she was about ready to slap me. 'What's the big deal?' she asked. She hadn't read it, didn't know who you were. We met for dinner and she tagged along to the bookstore. 'You're acting like a thirteen-year old,' she said."

"Did you bring it with you?" I asked. "I'll sign it when we get back to the house."

"Actually, you signed it that night."

"Oh."

"Yeah," she hemmed. "My friend said she wouldn't talk to me for a year if I didn't get back in line."

"I see."

"There was a pretty long line that night," she tried to help. "And I was near the end, of course."

"I saw you?"

She looked at me as though patting me on the head.

"You were tired."

I didn't care for that excuse. I had fallen for her at first sight when she arrived at the ranch. That first sight could not be second.

Sensing my bewilderment, she proposed an additional hypothesis.

"I had longer hair then."

Which was a promising idea I was prepared to latch onto, until she expanded on it.

"After I got my haircut, that friend of mine who went to the reading teased me about wanting to look like you."

Whether her friend was correct didn't matter.

What counted was that I had not noticed her before, when she looked less like me.

My shame pinballed between explanations. I rooted for ignorance over narcissism. I grounded myself by focusing on our surroundings and placing us in the small space we took up in it, the nanosecond in time, the speck of dust on the land, all in the interest of assuring myself this too shall pass.

But it was too soon for that to be of any comfort.

I made a snap decision to be relieved. My conundrum was solved. No more waffling between love and commerce. The puzzle was now strictly personal, made from pieces of vanity and caution.

"Shall I grow it out?" she interrupted my spiral.

"Huh?"

"My hair."

I laughed at myself and let it serve in appreciation of her joke.

"I'm sorry," I said. "I should not have put you in this position."

"I'm flattered."

"And I should not have put our organization in this position."

"No need to write a press release," she held up her hands. "I'm not taking any action. Not even a hashtag."

I found her even more attractive now that I wasn't attracted to her anymore. The hug she gave me on top of that hill was the missing element that unlocked the landscape's ability to melt the thin coat of sleaze which I had felt start to thicken.

We continued to spend time together. It may not have been the relationship I wished for when we first met, but it was a relationship that nonetheless had crossed a threshold from tension to serenity, like the great ones often do. I was more confident than before that we would stay in touch. She was more than a guest passing through.

Lee was of course delighted that our transition didn't include romance. I provided him with a watered-down version of our story that soft-pedaled the physical resemblance. The ending was all that mattered to him, though, so he wasn't interested in gloating over any particular plot twist that he saw coming.

Devon never knew. She was more boss than partner by then, retreating as far from the retreat as she could while maintaining the sort of amorphous, nebulous presence she had encouraged in me, and now exercised with me.

Our daily meetings, held wherever we happened to be at any given time, were winnowed down to weekly meetings in her office, then in a side room of the conference center after it was finished. Her reclusiveness was in part a product of age. Movement was becoming more painful. The way her limbs appeared to be lifted and lowered by invisible pulleys and ropes was reminiscent of my old patients, as were the noises she made, as though supplying sound effects for the phantom gears, squeaks and groans that occasionally emerged from the joints themselves.

"Someone called trying to get in touch with you," she mentioned at the conclusion of one of our meetings when Lee asked in closing if there was anything else, if we were forgetting anything.

"When?" I asked.

"A few days ago, I guess."

"Did they leave a name?"

"Not really. She said she was related to someone you took care of. Oh, what was it. The name. Something with an 'L'. Lori?"

"Libby?"

"That's it."

"Oh, Libby..." Lee's voice lilted with fond memories.

"What about her?" I was more concerned with the present.

"She didn't say. Wanted to talk to you about whatever it is."

"Did she leave a number?"

"It's on my desk somewhere."

I didn't ask if she could find it. I glared at her instead.

"Anything else?" Lee looked to finally end the meeting.

"Nope," Devon chirped.

I shook my head and kept staring at Devon, who either didn't notice or didn't care. She hoisted herself up and pieced her way through the door.

"Are you going to fetch that number?" Lee asked me when she was gone in a trail of deliberate motion and humming meant to conceal the creaking.

"Soon enough," I said while searching Libby's name on the web via my phone.

Her obituary was typical.

One quarter devoted to details of her life, and three quarters devoted to a list of those related to her who were still alive.

I showed Lee.

"That's a long list of relatives," he also noted the use of space.

"I never met even one of them."

"Survived by..." Lee meditated on the language of obituaries. "But remembered by?"

I estimated Devon had reached her office, that I had given her enough of a head start.

She found the number.

I took it without a word.

She neither called me out for my lack of manners, nor apologized for hers.

The woman related to Libby didn't answer. I left a voice mail message and took a walk to the site of the pond.

They had started to dig. Two backhoes worked on each end of the shallow hole, mechanically moaning back and forth as if taunting one another about their progress.

The woman called back as I watched them loudly burrow. I had to plug my free ear to hear her.

She was Libby's great niece, the granddaughter of her brother.

After we shared our identities, I told her I had looked up Libby's obituary, so she need not deliver the bad news.

"Thank you," she said. "I've had to do that a lot."

"I'm sorry I didn't call earlier. My director only gave me your message today."

"That's okay. Some people will probably never call back."

"I didn't see anything about a memorial in the notice. I hope that's what this is about."

"Yes, it is."

"So I didn't miss it?"

"No."

"And I'm invited?"

"Absolutely."

She provided the details and I thanked her for the information, thanked her for the invitation, thanked her for calling.

Before we hung up, I said "Thanks again."

I enjoyed my time on the ranch so much it never occurred to me that I was spending too much time there. Aside from the occasional errand and lunch with Lee, I had barely left the premises in almost a year. I had yet to be paid, and had yet to notice.

I asked Devon for money to attend Libby's memorial, but only after spending a restless forty-eight hours taking deep breaths and conjuring enough strength to utter the request. Her reaction was a relief, a refreshing departure from her grump phase. She laughed as she asked for my account number so she could make a transfer, and laughed even harder when I told her I didn't have an account.

"Maybe you really are some sort of mystic," she said. "What did you do, show up to your clients' door with a wooden bowl and spoon?"

"I had a bank account a while back, in a city I moved away from when I started elder care. Once I started living with people and eating with them, the money was sort of a bonus. They paid me in cash."

She grinned and shook her head as she reached under the desk to fiddle with her safe.

"Give her family my condolences," she cracked, tossing a stack of currency my way.

The trip felt like shifting positions in bed. I was already comfortable, but rolling over onto a fresh side offered a cooler slice of sheets and pillow, with a gentle stretch of the muscles.

Walking the streets of a big city for the first time since planning our retreat was disorienting for a few blocks, as though I had never before been surrounded by tall buildings and the engine noise of humanity, until a variety of breezes reoriented me to the experience: a warm gust rising up through a grate in the sidewalk, a brisk wind from a passing bus as I waited to cross at an intersection, and a chill of air conditioning blasting through the doors of a department store flung open by a customer saddled with shopping bags.

I saw why Libby didn't care to spend much time with most of the people I met at her funeral, but I appreciated them.

They lacked imagination. They were not the type who saw their stories as part of a larger story. They were not worried about their future. They remembered little of their past that didn't involve heavy drinking and getting into trouble. They thought nothing of death, even at a memorial. They relegated Libby to heaven and left it at that. They didn't know me. They were just what I needed.

I hung out with a gang of them who went bar-hopping after the service. We coupled cheap beer with generic spirits that came from large containers. We told every stupid joke we could remember and quoted scenes from movies and shows because they didn't have any stories about Libby. They would try to tell stories on each other every so often, but those stories were dull, and they would realize it halfway through and rush to the finish. Everyone would force a laugh then someone would ask if anyone had seen the recent Dave Chappelle special, or if anyone remembered that scene from *Step Brothers*, or that episode of *The Big Bang Theory*.

I knew I would never see them again. I had a blast.

•••

The immortal doesn't often wonder about his parents or siblings, if he had any. Who they might be, what they were like. His parents may have never found out about his condition, if either of them lived long enough to shepherd him into adulthood. He would move away when it started to dawn on anyone that something was wrong, or at least not right. Maybe it dawned on everyone. Maybe nobody ever said anything, but when he announced his plans to leave, everyone understood why that was a good idea, even if it took place in a time when families stuck together, and striking out on one's own would strike many as odd. But he would have to leave. It would be best for everyone. The immortal imagines what a family conversation sounded like. What language they spoke, what that language was capable of expressing. Maybe they just grunted at each other in a variety of tones, trying to use noises that normally communicated warnings or commands for a more complicated topic. Not that a vast vocabulary would help much. He was going to live for a long time, maybe forever. They were not. If they believed in everlasting life, they would have to trust it was coming later. If their faith wasn't utterly shaken, they could claim their route was preferable, that immortality was best lived in an invisible realm. Little of this would be spoken. He was happening, and his creators had no answers. No how, nor why. They were as frustrated as he was, maybe even as scared as he was. If they loved him. If they were scared for him rather than of him. His brothers and sisters may have been more jealous than scared. Why not them? Why was immortality limited to one child? Why brown hair, but not eternity? Looking back on something he cannot see, the immortal assumes he turned the question around. Why was he cursed while they were blessed? But back then, back when, before he cycled through the first average lifespan, he may not have been aware of the drawbacks. Maybe he was excited, and in turn apologetic or defensive toward his siblings. He secretly

100

gloated, and perhaps let his arrogance slip, or fly, as he left them to simmer in their envy, in their short-lived speck of existence. Though "speck" might be overstating their significance. A speck has a chance of discovery, of being remembered, and if he can't recall them, no one else has. If he had siblings. If he had parents.

Mildred was gone when I returned to the ranch. I could have accessed her contact information, but she left no note, sent me no text, so I didn't bother, since she clearly didn't want to be bothered. It was her hair all over again, the second time I saw her which I thought was the first time. I never noticed her in line at the bookstore when she needed to be noticed, when she was uncomfortable and unable to project the self-confidence I found comforting. Our situation in paradise was making her sad, but it suited me, so I tailored my perspective to fit my self-regard. I wanted to blame the book, the conferences, the retreat. My ego wasn't that big. But that's what someone with a big ego would think.

The conversations in the mornings and over dinner were still engaging. There were still plenty of interesting people at the retreat. We landscaped the area around the pond together, planted young willow trees that would soak up the water once the hole was filled and provide shade along the shoreline. We built platforms to jump from, fed the longhorns, prepared meals, but I missed having one person to review it all in a non-official capacity, to help me summarize what we were doing and what we were talking about. One person with whom to assess other people. One person to make me feel better about everyone else. The keeper of the mundane, of conversations that mean nothing other than what is being discussed, of moments soon forgotten that nonetheless contribute to a sense of having been someplace worthwhile.

That one. The one.

My lack of her made it easy to get back into character. I was never more detached and observant. As interesting as everyone was, as diligent in their work, and as much as I enjoyed their company, we seemed to be auditioning rather than interacting. Things we said were profound, our moments were accomplished, but to remember them would call on memorization rather than memory. I listened more closely to the birds than I did to the clients.

I thought of a passage in my book, which I rarely did by then, the part about the immortal being unable to dabble in small talk. He is so overwhelmed by awareness of how fleeting everything is that he can't be bothered with any little things. This was presented as one of the advantages of immortality. To be undisturbed by leaky faucets and what someone may think of you at work and the correct answer to whether a certain color looks good on your lover seemed liberating when I wrote it. But with Mildred gone, I realized it was just another curse.

•••

The immortal feels a kinship with animals. Not because his suspended state lends itself to any sort of unspoken connection or universal bond. No. He appreciates how animals stay the same. People change. Grooming, fashion, slang, technology, trends fluctuate. Human history is a tale of discovery and reinvention. Dogs, cats, and birds survive. Like the immortal. He sticks to the basics. He doesn't keep pets. He would go through thousands of them if he did. That's too many goodbyes. He instead enjoys the moments when he encounters animals in passing. He especially loves yellow Labradors, gray tabby cats, and crows, since they're all common species that tend to look alike. He imagines it's the same animal whenever he meets one. He calls every Lab "Sonny", every tabby "Spike", and every crow "Stretch". The same animal with a perpetual timeline running parallel to his, crossing paths on occasion to commiserate. "How have you been?" he says to Sonny as he rubs their head and chin while their owner looks on with a close-lipped smile. Only when the immortal is ready to move on does he say, "Still going, can you believe it?" Because saying anything beyond "good boy" or "good girl" to a dog in the presence of its owner inspires an overprotective tug on the leash. The immortal can say much more to the cats and crows, as there is never an owner nearby, and the conversation is almost always conducted from a distance, aside from the one in ten tabbies that approaches him and rolls around in the attention. "Feels good to be alive, doesn't it?" he'll coo to the cat right before rubbing its belly so it will attack his hand, which is the immortal's cue to say "to a point." He and Spike the tabby have been performing this routine for decades, possibly centuries. Once every three years or so they'll have an audience, usually a child or two waiting their turn to pet the kitty. The children laugh, probably at the act of Spike grabbing and munching on the immortal's hand rather than the comic timing of the dialogue, but he enjoys the laughter anyway.

It makes him feel less loony for eternally chuckling at his own joke. "We're a good team, Spike" he'll say before yielding to the children and saying so long to his partner until next time. He can't recollect touching a crow during one of their talks, but Stretch is a better listener than either Sonny or Spike. The crow looks interested in what he's saying. The longest conversations he has about immortality are with Stretch. There may be some hopping and cawing and fluttering onto different fence posts and suspension lines, but the neck cranes and the head cocks often enough when the immortal speaks to let him know he's being heard. They usually meet in a deserted section of a large parking lot where garbage has blown from the trash bins lashed to the light standards, or by the side of a lightly-traveled highway in a fallow field lined with telephone poles. He always ends their discussion with "Maybe someday we'll find out why." If Stretch happens to caw, trying to get the last word in, the immortal will continue, as though the crow asked him a question. "Why you and me are supposed to be here for so long," he answers. When he leaves those sessions with Stretch, he wonders about other animals whose purpose is unclear. Why are those penguins still in the Antarctic balancing their eggs and their babies on their feet under their bellies to keep them from freezing to death for months in twenty-four hour darkness? Would the Southern Ocean be so overrun with fish if the penguins disappeared? And what about wasps? Nasty bee impersonators with unlimited stingers and nothing to offer besides irritation and pain. He stops short of questioning the point of humans. It's too easy, done too often, and living forever makes him sensitive to overkill.

My favorite chore was watering the longhorns. It was the first task I ever performed at the ranch, so doing it a year later, amongst all the changes to the land, brought me back to the days when I thought maybe Devon might publish my book. I remember being disappointed the first time we made the rounds that the herd wasn't happy to see us, as they would be if we were driving a pickup truck or ATV with bales of hay or bags of feed piled in back. With food they would speed walk behind us, heads and horns swaying, the line growing longer with each clique we passed.

So I was excited to see them all gathered around the water station farthest from headquarters on the foggy morning I discovered the body.

My excitement tempered as I drew closer through the mist and realized reaching the spigot and tank may be challenging. I had never ordered them around, nor seen Devon have to. I wondered if tone of voice was key, or if I needed to slap one of them on their hindquarters. They solved the problem by parting when I approached, clearing a path without a sound other than their breathing, and the muffled snaps of damp dead grass buckling under their hooves.

I recognized him, but could not remember his name. He was a recent arrival, filling the spot vacated by Mildred with a serene presence that had me wondering why he felt a need to join our knot of gabby high-achievers. Half his face was purple, with an especially deeper shade indicating where the blow landed that started his end.

I liked to leave my phone behind on the early morning lap around the grounds, so I started walking to the house, then jogging, then sprinting once I could see it.

Breakfast was about to be served. I waved and clenched a smile as I slowed past the kitchen, finally catching my breath in large gulps outside Devon's office and sweating so profusely I could barely grip the knob and close the door behind me.

"I'd get on you about knocking," she looked up from behind her desk, "But you appear to have some breaking news."

"The new guy," I heaved between breaths. "I don't know his name. Real quiet."

"I haven't memorized his name, either. What about him?"

"He's dead."

"Who else knows?"

I took several breaths to wonder why that was her first response.

"Nobody," I finally answered. "As far as I know. I found him by the water station closest to the gate. Looks like he was hit in the head, so somebody may have been with him."

"By the water station?"

"Yes."

"Was the herd there?"

"They were surrounding him."

"Could have been one of them," Devon picked up her phone. "Let's hope so."

She tapped on the screen while giving me an order.

"I need you to go to breakfast and see if anyone is acting suspicious or saying anything."

"Are you calling the police?"

"No," she put the screen to her ear.

"Why not?"

She started talking to the person she dialed rather than answer me.

"Hello," she said to whomever it was. "Time to earn your keep."

She listened to the person on the other end and shooed me away while murmuring "uh huh" to whatever she heard.

I didn't notice anything at breakfast.

I wasn't capable of noticing anything.

I had a half-purple head on my mind.

I sat on the edge of the patio with a plate of home fries pretending to take in a view that was hidden behind a churning wall of morning fog.

An overheard conversation dropped me back into the present I was having such a hard time assessing, an exchange between two women one table behind me.

"That new guy asked me to do shrooms with him last night."

"You too?"

I would like to claim I had the strength to restrain myself from breaking character and wheeling around to gasp "Really?"

But I was so surprised that I froze.

"Really?" one of the women said it for me.

"And pretty much every other woman here."

"Oh my God."

"Seriously. Like some frat party."

"Did anyone take him up on it?"

"Are you kidding?"

"Probably why he's not at breakfast."

I stood up to deliver the results of my accidental investigation to Devon.

"Oh, hi Luca," one of them said. "Didn't see you there."

"Like a spirit," said the other.

I smiled but failed to laugh.

"Sorry," I said. "I couldn't help but hear what you were talking about. I need to talk to Devon about this."

"You're not going to kick him out or anything, are you?"

"He seems harmless enough. Just lame."

"He's excited to be here," one said.

"Who can blame him?" the other closed their case by beckoning toward the valley, where the fog had lifted.

"Thank you," I nodded and sidled away. "We'll take that into consideration."

When I arrived back at Devon's office, one of the guests was sitting across the desk from her. He was one of our original members.

"You know Michael," Devon greeted me.

"Of course," I tried to conceal my discombobulation. "We nail-gunned about half the frame of the conference center together."

"It's okay," Devon held up her hand. "He knows."

"He does?"

Michael nodded.

"He's a ringer," she said, as though it was an admission.

"What do you mean?" I asked.

"He's worked for me before. Though he is genuinely interested in changing his life. Aren't you, Michael?"

He nodded again, but with a slight shrug this time. He swiped a wallet that was on Devon's desk and started to study its contents.

"What does he do?" I was under the impression I wasn't supposed to address him directly.

"You don't remember," she remarked. "That's by design. He blends in."

"A lawyer?" I guessed.

Devon raised her eyebrows and blew out a single-syllable laugh.

"You're losing your touch, counselor," she teased him.

"There are a lot of lawyers here," he defended himself, still burrowing through the wallet.

"See how little Michael talks?" she asked me. "He's a special kind of lawyer, the kind who never sets foot in a courtroom, or even a conference room for that matter. But he's working on it. He's here for the same reason as anyone else. Self-improvement. Doing the 'Should Shuffle.'"

He suspended his search. They exchanged grins.

"In the meantime, though," she continued, "He's here to help. Working in the same capacity for us as he always has."

She didn't follow through on what that was.

"Have a seat, Luca," she invited me over instead. "Stop standing by the door like Boo Radley."

I obeyed. They waited until I was settled to proceed.

"Do you have any information for us?" she asked.

"He was looking for someone to do shrooms with last night."

"Shrooms?" Devon groaned. "As in psilocybin? Psychedelics?"

"I assume."

"Good Lord," She ranted. "Will the 60s just die already? It's a retreat, not a time machine. Was he wearing a dashiki?"

I knew she wasn't really asking, but answered anyway. Her mentorship still inspired a waning sense of loyalty in me.

"Jeans and a sweatshirt," I assured her. "Also, everyone blew him off, apparently. All the women, at least. If that makes you feel any better."

Devon and Michael looked at one another and indeed seemed to feel very good.

"A blow to the head and drugs in his system," she fed him a partial summary.

"And no witnesses," he fed her the rest.

"What a gift," she concluded.

They appeared to forget I was there.

"What's going on here?" I reminded them.

Devon faced me while Michael made some mental calculations.

"This is our fork in the road," she explained. "The point where we decide if we can take care of it ourselves, or if we go the traditional route."

"Meaning call the police," I confirmed.

"And the other lawyers," she clarified.

I looked at Michael, who was still looking inside his head, then back at Devon.

"So..." I already knew the answer. "Which path are we taking this time?"

"Michael?" she deferred to counsel.

He came out of his trance.

"Pack all his things in his luggage," he said to me. "Leave nothing behind. He didn't bring much."

"You were already there?"

"Right after Devon called me."

"So that's his wallet."

"Would he be that fascinated with his own?" Devon muttered.

"Devon will drive you to the front gate," Michael said. "Don't let anyone see you enter and exit his room."

"Wait a second..." I stood up.

"You're already involved," he said. "Save your breath."

I stared at Devon.

"Your book has been the cornerstone of this project," she said.

"But it's your company that put it together," I hissed. "Your property, your ideas. Your insane, fucked-in-the-head ideas."

Devon sighed.

"You're still not very well-known," she said.

"So?"

"You will be if we take the road more traveled. If we call the authorities and tell them a wannabe hippie mistook our corporate retreat for a commune, ate magic mushrooms, and tried to hug a longhorn."

Michael giggled. Devon continued.

"That report would leak, and the stories springing from it will always mention you and your book. You'll be a punchline."

"It'll fade. People move on to the next weird story within days."

"Not for you. When you introduce yourself, apply for a job, people will wonder where they've heard your name before. Maybe they'll ask you if they can't figure it out for themselves at first. Then maybe you'll lie, hoping they don't look it up later. It'll be like having a criminal record."

"I will have a criminal record if I go along with your masquerade."

"You will have committed a crime," Michael chimed in. "But there will be no record of it."

"And think of that poor bastard being mourned by the herd right now," Devon took charge again. "What an undignified way to go. He wouldn't want anyone to know. We're doing him a favor. This is what he would want."

"Whatever his name is," I quipped.

"I'm not pretending to know him," she fired back. "But I know people. Our legacies matter to us. Shame is its own kind of death."

I stared at the floor, unable to meet their eyes.

"We appreciate how difficult this is," Michael said. "How sudden and surprising. But we know what we're doing, and we're running out of time. Please pack his bags and meet Devon in the driveway."

"Where's his room?" I asked the floor.

"Second story," Devon answered. "Third door on the opposite side of the atrium from yours."

I left and steered clear of the breakfast service.

Michael was right. He didn't have much. Another pair of jeans, a pair of khakis, three pairs of shorts, a bunch of shirts, only one of them collared, another sweatshirt, a windbreaker, and a pair of nice sneakers that he probably used as dress shoes. He had a toothbrush, toothpaste, deodorant, a bag of disposable razors, and a can of shaving cream. Everything fit in the one bag he brought, which looked like it could have baseball gear or tennis rackets in it, instead of his worldly possessions.

I sat on the edge of the bed and scanned the empty, furnished room. I wasn't worried about leaving anything behind. If I was searching, it was for a sense of remorse, of sadness. Something to honor someone who was about to disappear.

My phone shook. It was a text from Devon.

"Ready?"

I wrote that I was.

The engine was running when I sat in the passenger seat. I kept his bag on my lap.

"Want to know his name?" she handed me two pieces of paper stapled together. "It's on page two. The credit card receipt."

Page one was a train boarding pass.

"I'm taking a train?"

"It'll help you relax," she said as she put us in gear and rolled slowly from the pavement to the gravel. "I'll cover for you at the sessions today and have Lee sit in tomorrow morning, maybe the evening, if you and Michael aren't back by then."

"Does Lee know what's going on?"

"No. You're going to another funeral for another patient. The same story we're going to tell the guests."

I glanced at the boarding pass.

"We're not going to make it all the way to Seattle and back by tomorrow evening."

"You're not going all the way. And you're not coming back on the train."

I was about to ask a question, but she stopped me.

"Let Michael explain. It's his plan, and he seems quite proud of it."

He was parked to the side of the gravel road at a point where if lines were drawn to it from the watering station and the front gate they would meet to form a right angle. He stood beside the car, the kind of silver sedan people drive in their morning commute.

"See you tomorrow," Devon said to me while waving at him.

She started her U-turn the moment I closed the door.

"Throw the bag in the back seat," Michael directed me. "The trunk is full."

I walked around to the passenger side and followed orders.

"Does he have a long coat in there?" he asked as he took his place behind the wheel.

"Just a short one."

"That's okay. I've got one you can wear."

He checked the battery level of a cell phone plugged into the charger.

I waited for him to explain how the coat fit whatever we were about to do.

We were at the gate within a minute. I jumped out to open and shut it. I climbed back in and sat down. We drove toward town, and still I waited.

We stopped at the shopping center where locals ran their errands and tourists came when they needed something besides wine, tapas, and sheep's milk ice cream.

"What size shoe do you wear?" he asked as we pulled into a parking space near the shoe store unit.

"Ten."

"I'll be right back."

I slumped into a sarcastic thumbs-up but didn't reach the part where I raise my thumbs. He was out of the car by then.

We were one of four cars in the parking lot close to the storefronts, which had just opened. The employees were all parked on the far end. Michael was the only customer I could see though the window. He took a quick lap to find what he needed and pay.

He returned with a box and handed it to me.

"He was wearing these. Put them on."

"Any chance you're going to tell me what we're doing?"

"You haven't asked. I thought maybe you wanted to let it play out, see what happens next."

"I've had enough surprises this morning."

"Whatever," he exhaled. "You're almost caught up, anyway."

"Sorry if I'm making this less fun."

"After I drop you off, I'm going to drive ahead along the route and find a small station close to the end that doesn't have any cameras, or not many of them. It's not that big a deal as long as we get the shoes right and cover your outfit with the coat."

"I'm a body double."

"There's a camera at the station here, aimed at the depot, so if you turn immediately after walking out the door and head to one end of the platform, we'll be fine."

"I don't look like him."

"You're close enough in height and have the same hair color. That's all we need. The videos are grainy, and so are people's memories. If anyone who interacts with you is questioned, they'll give the same vague description, and everyone will accept it because they want to solve the mystery."

He unplugged the cell phone and handed it to me.

"This is his phone. Doesn't get much action. He exchanges texts once in a while with a friend nicknamed Rabble. I think it's a woman. Anyway, keep an eye on it. Respond if she texts. Keep it short. I'm going to send you a message on that phone after you cross the Oregon-Washington border. It may be a text, might be an email. Depends on what kind of device I'm able to borrow. You're not going to recognize the number. The message will be cryptic. Something like, "I got it. Next stop." Reply with "Can't it wait for Seattle?" To which I'll say "Now or never." When you get off, leave the phone behind. Stick it between the seat cushions like you didn't mean to. I won't be in the parking lot. Start walking from the station and I'll find you. Then we'll head back to the ranch."

"What about the body?"

"I'll have already taken care of that. See if the shoes fit."

I unwrapped them and put my old shoes in the box. The news ones were comfortable. I curled and uncurled my toes, pointed my feet and swiveled them.

"Is anyone going to find him?" I asked.

"I'll give them a chance. Maybe fifty-fifty."

"What kind of place are you going to put him in?"

"A place you would expect. I'll have to wait and see what's available."

He started the car, put it in reverse, and looked behind us.

I speculated on the story that our actions were supposed to tell.

"Man gets off train to score drugs and the deal takes a bad turn."

"Too cliché?" he asked as he shifted gears and faced forward.

"Standard narratives are comforting," I answered. "We want to make sense of the world, and they help us do that."

"I wasn't really asking," he said. "But thank you."

We drove to the station in silence, which made me think of how long the drive back was going to be.

"The train isn't due for a few hours," he said when we arrived. "But I need a head start. The coffee shop down the street is pretty good."

He handed me a twenty dollar bill.

"See you in some small town in Washington," I waved with the twenty as I took it.

"Grab your coat and your bag," he reminded me.

Neither of which was mine.

Michael kept the wallet. It would be buried along with its owner. I wondered if the money he gave me was from the wallet. It would make sense to take the cash if we were trying to simulate a crooked drug deal.

Before I shut the door I leaned in to ask him a question.

"Have you ever killed anyone?"

"I fix things," he replied. "It's a hard job. All killing does is create more problems that need fixing."

It occurred to me later as I paid my bill at the coffee shop with what I thought of as the dead man's cash that Michael never quite answered the question.

I wondered if he would have enough time to do what he needed to do, but the train ride revealed what a luxurious amount of time was going to be available.

The train never seemed to reach top speed. There was often a curve to navigate, or a crossing that required caution, or a station. When we ran parallel to a freeway, the vehicles sped past us, even those in the slow lane. We were at our fastest when the scenery was most beautiful. The background would hold still. The mountains, lakes, and clouds were immovable, while things right in front of us were a blur. Then we would ease into a town, through a part of it that didn't have money and influence to keep the tracks away from their backyard, and the foreground would dominate. Plastic bags and cardboard boxes that once held objects used by those in the powerful neighborhoods swirled and shook in our turbulence.

When the conductor passed through to check my ticket, I made steady eye contact with her and smiled. If anyone asked her about the man I was portraying, I wanted her recollection to be positive. I wanted to pay tribute his memory.

During one of our more beautiful interludes, as we descended from the Oregon Cascades, I felt a phone quiver at my hip. Service had been scarce through the mountains, so I figured it was a message sent earlier and only now received, and that passengers all across the train were also getting buzzed at the same time.

It wasn't my phone.

It was his.

"How's the retreat?" Rabble asked.

I responded without hesitation.

"Not what I thought it was going to be."

"Sorry."

"I left. On my way home."

"Call me when you get back."

"Will do," I wrote, but didn't send right away.

I stared at the words and came closest to crying over a man I hardly knew but whose life was now forever attached to mine. When I pressed the send button, it felt like sliding his body into the sea.

•••

The immortal likes to travel, but doesn't do it often for pleasure. He usually does it to move, to stay ahead of familiarity and recognition. He appreciates the lengthy amount of time spent with people he won't meet again. Small talk doesn't resonate with him. Living for thousands of years makes the talk too small to see the point. People on a long trip seem to understand this as well. Their relationships being transitory, they unburden themselves rather than fill space. So the immortal hears confessions. He remembers a woman on an airplane who told him she found it hard to look at her husband after cancer surgery smeared half his face when she knew it was coming, when she had stuck by him and motivated him, found inspiration in him, but had a hard time making eye contact with him after he recovered, and made up excuses to spend time away, as though she was having an affair, when all she was doing was spending time alone being ashamed of herself. A man on a cross-country bus said he really did have an affair, multiple affairs, with people like the woman's husband, people with limbs removed and prominent scars, because he thought it made them feel good, even though he had a feeling it made him feel better. The revelations differ in the details, but are always about whether a selfless act has a trace of self-interest, or if a selfish act can be morally spun. The fellow travelers sense the immortal is someone who will listen, who will not be surprised by anything they say. A long ride is the rare timespan when the immortal feels a kinship with people. He would do it more often if he could afford to.

•••

I didn't mind the hours of silence on the drive south. I was able to rehearse what I wanted to say to Devon. Sleep never followed. There was too much to think about. What I had done, and what needed to be done.

Michael and I spoke only twice. Once when we stopped to dump the bag and I offered to drive for a spell, which he refused, and then when we stopped to eat in a twenty-four hour diner at midnight, where I asked him what kind of law he wanted to practice after he finished the retreat.

"Probate," he answered.

I laughed, twenty-four hours of tension barking out of me.

Michael may have also laughed loudly if he wasn't so embarrassed by my overreaction, which vibrated across the nearly-empty dining room.

The drive passed in different shades of darkness. He picked me up two miles away from the station I left at sunset under a blushing twilight sky, we cruised at top speed in the pitch black of empty freeways at midnight, and drove up the gravel road of the ranch in the gray before sunrise.

When he parked the car, he pushed a button and locked all the doors when I tried to open mine.

"Like it never happened," he said.

I nodded, holding my gaze through the windshield.

"Look at me," he insisted.

"Got it," I faced him. "Like it never happened."

"As it is with everything eventually," he grinned.

I was supposed to catch the reference. The line did sound familiar. It could have been a variation on a theme from any number of sources. But he pressed on and provided some clarity.

"The immortal cries out to the universe, 'Why?' and he hears an echo rather than an answer, the same question repeated over and over and over and realizes it's not his voice echoing, it's all the other shaken souls in the universe shouting the same word and hearing nothing besides the sound of one another's voices rattling around the space that is just that, space."

I grinned, or at least tried to.

"Your book means a lot to me," he explained. "Made me feel a lot better about the kind of work I was doing, but also question it. Weird, huh?"

I elongated my face in agreement.

"I wanted to say something before," he continued. "But I was supposed to keep a low profile, and even if I wasn't on duty, I'd hate to come across as some pushy fanboy."

"I wouldn't have thought anything..."

"Then since yesterday, when I finally had the chance, we were too caught up in my work."

"We certainly were."

"So..." he improvised now that he had finished his script. "Here we are. Just wanted to say thanks. For everything."

"You're welcome," I said.

"I guess," I thought, leaving the car feeling as though I had been on a clumsy date rather than an elaborate deception.

I slept longer than the drive had taken.

Maybe even longer than the train ride.

Before speaking with Devon, I shared my plan with Lee at our favorite haunt over a late lunch.

He was disappointed, but supportive.

"All of our conversations lately are about all the effort you put in to stay," he said. "It reminds me of couples counseling at church. It's important to work on a relationship, but when it becomes nothing but sweat, then it might be time to move on."

"Thank you for understanding."

The server brought our iced tea and asked if we were ready. As was so often the case, and for which she often teased us, we were not. Too busy talking. We asked for another minute. She looked at her watch and pretended to set the timer.

"I wonder," Lee signaled the return of our conversation, "Do the funerals have more to do with this than you're letting on?"

"Funerals?" I couldn't place the plural.

"Libby," he reminded me, "And the one you just got back from. What was their name?"

The first name of a former patient I could think of was a man named Joe.

"Do you think maybe Libby and Joe are tugging you back to your old job?"

"Maybe."

I thought of Joe, who I assumed was still alive. He and I didn't get along. He was the kind of man who challenges the conventional wisdom that anger is unhealthy by living on bitterness for a hundred years plus.

"You're helping people here, too," Lee put in a final plea.

"I'm using people," I shook my head. "Using them to feed my ego."

"There's always a little self-gratification in helping others. It makes us feel good."

"Look at Mildred," I talked over his assurances. "I only noticed her when she showed up looking more like me. And the lengths we go to in order to keep the spaces filled and keep the gears turning on this machine, this plantation disguised as a self-help program."

I lost him on that last point.

"All we do is accept applications," he maintained.

I moved on.

"I should have been content with your praise," I said. "I should have corresponded with you, and the two or three other fans who may have emerged, and kept working at my job that actually helps people. I should have been content with that."

"There is no should," he echoed the gist of so many of our conversations. "Only 'is' and 'was'. You made your choice. Now you're making another one. I hope it brings you peace."

I grabbed a menu and raised it like a shield, uncomfortable with Lee sounding so pastorly with me. When I read the items, I felt hungrier than I had in days, as though I could eat everything listed, and then order another round of it all.

I lowered the menu and looked at him.

"I'm going to miss you, Lee."

"Perhaps you can make some guest appearances at the ranch," he suggested.

"That might be nice, but I suspect Devon won't want anything to do with me."

"I'll wear a lot of that," Lee commiserated. "I pushed for you."

"Sorry."

"I would do it again."

"Thank you."

We had been to that restaurant dozens of times. I had two or three dishes that I rotated as my order. For my last visit, I decided to order something different, if for no other reason than to cause a stir with our server, and give us something to joke about.

Speaking with Devon involved some joking around, but the jokes were primarily intended to harm rather than humor.

I suggested we take a walk. It was yet another lovely afternoon to be outdoors, a spectacular late fall day of sunshine cool enough without any help from even the slightest breeze, but really I wanted to insure our conversation remain private. She, however, insisted on conducting our meeting in her office, so I carried on under the assumption she was recording us.

"I'm not concerned about your leaving," she said. "I have plenty of authors in the stable to keep the IPA going. Big, fading names ready to jump at the chance to come out here for a week and feel important. I'm worried about what you're going to do after you're gone."

"I thought I passed my loyalty test."

"The real test happens when people start to look for him, and if they find him. I'd prefer you stick around until all that passes, and you learn to live with whatever you want to call the feelings you'll have about it."

"And you'll be able to tell when I've reached that point?"

"Yes."

"Because you're such a brilliant analyst."

She smirked.

I was tired of her doing that.

"Still brilliant?" I blended my thoughts on her expression with my thoughts on her profession. "Or is that in the past?"

She appeared to sustain a hit. Small as it was, I couldn't recall having that effect on her. It was exciting.

"When was the last time you had a patient?" I swung harder. "You're more of a conference organizer at this point. A party planner."

"A publisher," she hit back. "A brand."

"A con artist."

"The Should Business is a luxury item," she leaned into her desk. "A pastime of the leisure class. They're not dumb. I'm not exploiting anyone. I'm meeting a demand. I'm no worse than a speedboat salesman, or a couture handbag designer."

Her breathing labored.

I felt guilty. My plan was to go back to caring for the elderly, and here I was tormenting one of them.

"Forgive me," I said. "I'm out of sorts, and now I'm out of line."

She laughed herself into a coughing fit.

"My God," she rasped as she came out of it. "How am I supposed to trust you out there if you can't even deal with teasing an old lady for a few seconds?"

"I was hoping to buy your peace of mind."

She raised her eyebrows, then cough-laughed again.

"You don't have a bank account," she managed to slip through the hacks. "I haven't been able to pay you."

"And you don't have to," I competed with her latest fit. "Donate all past and future royalties from the book to some of the non-profits our guests work for, or started."

I handed her a list from my pocket.

"This way I'll know some good came from my time here, and will continue to."

She was intrigued.

"If I let it," I added.

"If you keep your mouth shut."

"I've become very good at that while pretending to be a sage."

"Sales are slowing down," she weighed the offer.

"My disappearance may give them a bump. Develop a myth to feed on."

"Slap another layer on an already-confusing book."

"People will read even more into it. Season the pages with my vanishing."

"So you're going to change your identity again," she confirmed.

"Again?"

She smiled.

"Yes," she took pride in her awareness. "The only thing I don't know is how many times."

"Only once. When I became a legal adult."

"I would have guessed more. You're the immortal, after all."

It was a bigger reveal, but she gloated less. She may have even regretted bringing it up.

I was compelled to put her at ease.

"I've read that most authors imagine themselves as the characters in their book," I noted.

"But you're taking this to another level. I mean, look at your name. C'mon. Luca? Last Universal Common Ancestor?"

"What do you mean?"

"L-U-C-A. Last Universal Common Ancestor. The name scientists give to the organism all living things are related to. The tap root of the tree of life. The origin they're searching for."

"That's interesting," I considered pretending she was right. "And I'm flattered you think I could be so smart. But I named myself after that old Susanne Vega song about the kid who gets abused."

"Doesn't she spell that Luka with a 'k'?"

"I didn't want to be too obvious."

"There was a time when you valued subtlety?"

I matched her smile.

"I should have made the character a woman, like you wished. She would have provided better cover."

She paused, filling the space with suspicion, then drained it slowly.

"I don't mean any of this literally," she said. "Let's be clear. Your book isn't an autobiography. It's a story you tell yourself to feel better about your life. Your picture isn't on anyone's wall, or on their desk, or in their wallet. Not even after all that's happened this year. You're in a lot of pictures, but always next to a stranger, on their social media feed. You wrote the story down to prove you existed, and in case it never found an audience, to rationalize the possibility of nobody remembering you, since the message is how none of that matters."

I let her think her words were sinking in.

"I'm sorry I was such a disappointment," I said when the time seemed right. "I wish my work could have done more to preserve your legacy, and your husband's. Maybe even broaden it."

"I was too old to go in a new direction," she crafted an apology of her own. "One of the rare benefits of being my age is giving less of a shit about what people think. It's one of those connections between old age and childhood that hack psychologists like to point out. But it's also why someone my age should no longer be in charge of a business, especially their own. Especially a business so attached to their name."

She drifted, thinking perhaps of the man who shared her name.

"If you do squeal," she redirected her attention to me. "Wait until after I die. It'll keep my name out there a little longer."

She held out her hand.

I shook it.

"If you ever need a live-in nurse," I sealed our deal. "I never change my number."

She smirked again, but I didn't mind this time.

I spent one more day grinning and nodding at everyone, offering cryptic advice when asked, and contributing applause, along with everyone else, as water was unleashed into the pond through three different water cannons.

Devon and Lee stood together on the shore opposite me. The three of us silently acknowledged one another while the cannons roared. Everyone stood transfixed by the rising tide. The longhorns joined them, drawn by the sound. I walked back to the house to gather my belongings and disappear.

I encountered nobody along the way in the still evening air of autumn. The house, what I almost called home, was likewise empty. Like summer camp, the end was palpable not only thanks to the weather, but the sense it was too good to last.

•••

The immortal takes in a lovely sky. A pink evening sky streaked with clouds. An unfiltered night sky with stars exploding from the spine of the Milky Way. An orange morning sky reacquainting itself with the life it touches. A blue afternoon sky reaching higher than the others. The immortal takes in a lovely sky and feels like he is part of a larger animal, which is how he feels when he feels best, how he makes peace with forever.

Also by Sean Boling

The Current Mr. Orr
Devin's Best Afterlife
Once in Two Lifetimes
Revenge and Wellness in the Sweet Hereafter

Standalone
Cut Flowers
Abraham the Anchor Baby Terrorist
Pigs and Other Living Things
The Summer of Our Foreclosure
Satellite Campus
A Charter to That Other Place
The Latest Version of My Love Story
Show Them What They Won
The Name Field
Should
Moral Adjacent
Over Here We Have

About the Author

Sean lives with his family in Templeton, California. He teaches English at Cuesta College.

www.ingramcontent.com/pod-product-compliance
Lightning Source LLC
Chambersburg PA
CBHW062218150726
47991CB00006B/2327